THE ALIEN IN THE GARAGE

AND OTHER STORIES

THE ALIEN IN THE GARAGE

AND OTHER STORIES

ROB KEELEY

Matador
5 Weir Road
Kibworth Beauchamp
Leicester LE8 0LQ, UK
Tel: (+44) 116 279 2299
Fax: (+44) 116 279 2277
Email: books@troubador.co.uk
Web: www.troubador.co.uk/matador

ISBN 978 1848765 795

British Library Cataloguing in Publication Data.
A catalogue record for this book is available from the British Library.

Typeset in 11pt Book Antiqua by Troubador Publishing Ltd, Leicester, UK
Printed and bound in Great Britain by TJI Digital, Padstow, Cornwall

Matador is an imprint of Troubador Publishing Ltd

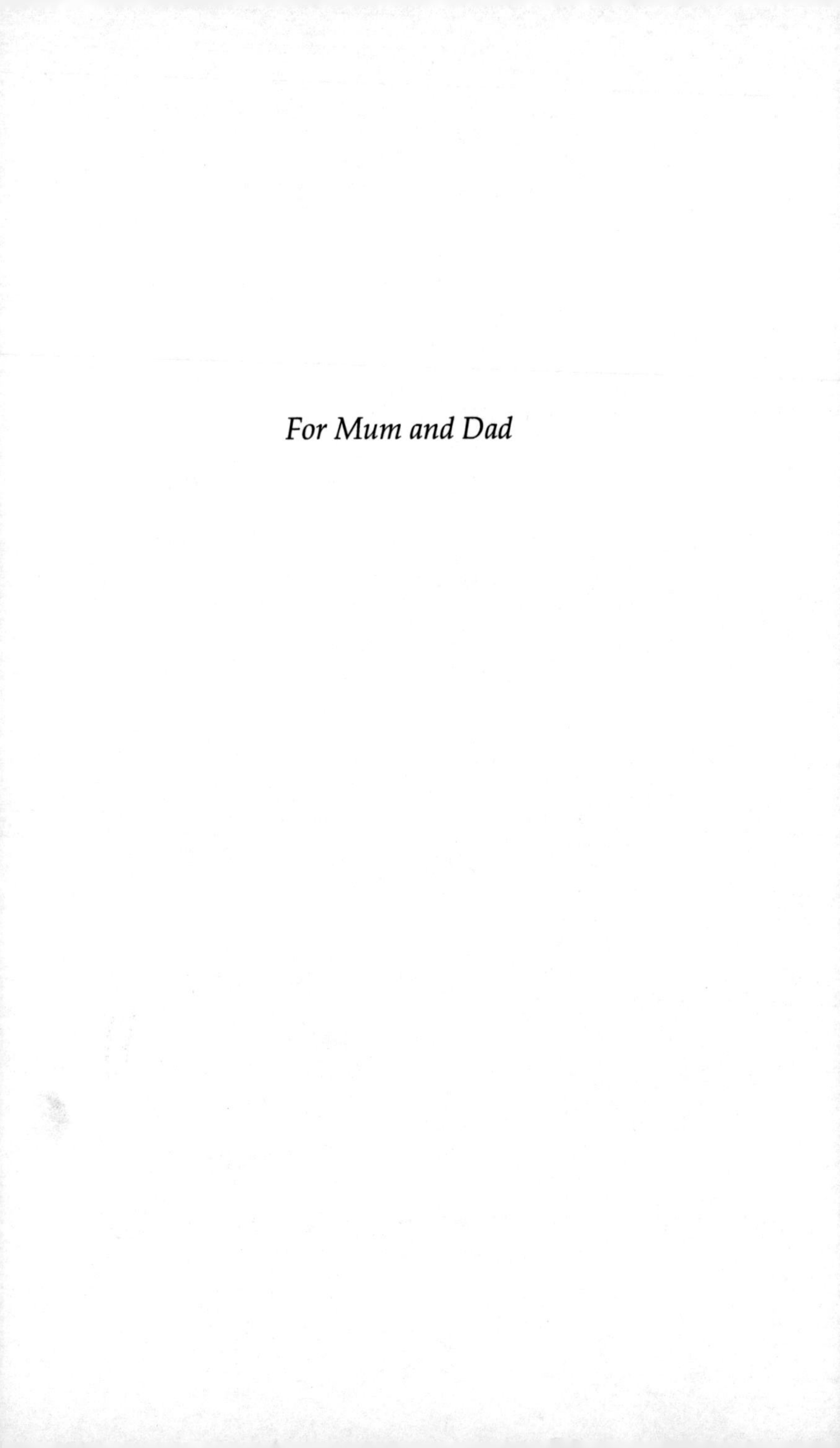

For Mum and Dad

Contents

The Alien in the Garage

"Neil!"

Neil groaned as he heard the loud, shrill voice.

The living room door opened. Jamie's round, freckled face appeared.

"Where's the biscuits?"

"The tin's on the top shelf." Neil struggled to balance the guitar he was holding, trying to find a comfortable position on the sofa. "Where it always is."

"I can't reach it!" Jamie whined.

Neil rolled his eyes. He put the guitar down.

"I'm trying to practise, Jamie!" He got up and followed his little brother into the kitchen. "What do you want them for, anyway? Mum's going to be home soon, we're going to have our tea."

He moved to the shelves.

"I want them for the alien!"

Neil stopped suddenly. He stared at Jamie.

"You what?"

"The alien!" Jamie repeated determinedly. "The alien in the garage."

"The alien." Annoyed as he was to be interrupted, Neil felt the corner of his mouth begin to twitch. "There's an alien. In our garage?"

"*Yeah!*" Jamie's face set in a frown, as if it were obvious. "He's waiting for a spaceship to pick him up."

Neil was definitely smirking now.

"And he wants custard creams?" He reached up for the biscuit tin.

"He's hungry!" Jamie insisted.

"OK." Neil handed the tin to Jamie with a grin. "So we've got an alien out there now? The dragon's gone, has he?"

"The dragon was *weeks* ago!" Jamie took the tin firmly. "I've been looking after the alien all week."

"Go on then, mate." Neil ruffled Jamie's hair, knowing his brother hated it when people did that. "Take the alien his biscuits."

"Ta." Jamie opened the back door and disappeared.

Smiling to himself, Neil returned to the living room.

Jamie was getting worse. The dragon had only been the last. A month ago, Jamie had said there was a spaceman in his wardrobe. Then there had been the fairy princess at the bottom of the garden. And last Christmas, Santa Claus had got stuck on the roof.

What was it with kids now? Neil was sure *he* hadn't been like that.

Anyway.

Neil took up the guitar again and began.

Two chords later, the door reopened.

"Neil!"

"What." Neil turned to Jamie, tight-lipped.

"Can I have some cushions?"

"Cushions?" repeated Neil.

"For the alien!" Jamie asked. "I've only got that old armchair out there. It'd be so much more comfy for him."

"For Pete's sake!" Neil grabbed two cushions from the other end of the sofa and hurled them at Jamie. "I've got to learn this piece, Jamie! I'm getting tested tonight. I can't go on playing *The James Bond Theme* and the snooker music forever!"

"He's got to get some sleep," Jamie protested. "He's got a long journey later."

"On the spaceship?" Neil asked wearily.

Jamie nodded solemnly.

"His planet's light years away from Earth."

"Go on." Neil grabbed another cushion from the adjacent chair and chucked it at his brother. "Get back to him. It. Whatever. And let me get on!"

"Ta." Half-hidden behind the pile, Jamie hurried back to the door and was gone.

Neil shook his head.

Soon, Jamie would have enough furniture out there to set up house on his own.

It wasn't that Neil minded his little brother building a den. In fact, Neil remembered, he'd had one himself a few years ago. Since they'd got rid of the car, the garage had only been used for storage, and it had a window, and another exit out of the back that was never locked, in the daytime. It was a perfectly safe place for Jamie to play.

But why did Jamie have to fill it with all these crazy made-up creatures?

It wouldn't have been so bad if he didn't use them as an excuse to get whatever he wanted out there. On his birthday, he'd asked for a TV/DVD player, so he could watch telly in the garage with the dragon. And he'd been given one. Now, he wanted the whole tin of biscuits, and half the living room cushions, for an alien.

At least the alien was leaving tonight.

Neil shuddered suddenly. What alien?

He was getting as bad as Jamie.

Trying to get aliens out of his head, he returned to guitar practice.

E minor. OK.

He plucked a chord.

"NEIL!"

Neil shot to his feet with an exclamation a lot worse than "For Pete's sake!" The guitar went flying and hit the floor with a loud *clonk!*

"That's rude," said Jamie. "Can I borrow your *Doctor Who* DVD? I thought it might be useful for him. And I'll take some magazines."

"Right!" Neil leapt for the coffee table, grabbed every magazine in sight and started to bombard his little brother with them.

"I thought he could learn something about Earth from them," Jamie explained. "No, not *Men Only*! That's Dad's. And if I can have the TV paper, we can see what's on…"

"Oh, *shut up*, will you!" Neil glowered at Jamie. "Look, Jamie, we all know you've got a den out there! You don't need to make up all these stories!"

"What stories?" Jamie looked hurt.

"Oh, go on." Neil picked up his guitar and sat down. "Go on. Get out. And just… leave it for a bit, will you? Give me a break."

Quietly, Jamie left the room. His eyes looked big and sad.

Neil sat down again, and took a long, deep breath.

He felt rotten now. But Jamie really could drive you round the bend at times.

He returned, as best he could, to his music.

Aliens! Honestly.

* * * *

Carrying the magazines carefully, Jamie walked up the little path from the back door, and opened the rear door of the garage.

The alien was inside, with his feet up on the table, on a cushion, on a pile of boxes, and on another old chair. Four pairs of feet in total. He had a custard cream in one hand, a can of orangeade in the other, and a copy of the A-Z in the other. One of his heads was reading the A-Z, and the other was watching Jamie's television.

He sat there, a magnificent creature in dark purple, his eight legs half-filling the small garage. He looked, to Jamie, like a cross between a tarantula and a gigantic plum.

Both heads and all four mouths smiled at Jamie as he entered.

"Weghfyytyfhfhfsijjgiorjiogjjgfijgijgijgirjigjrijgiirjgi jrigjijigjierjg…"

"I can't understand you." Jamie put the magazines down on an old coffee table that stood in front of the alien's battered armchair. "Can you put the translator thingie on again please?"

The alien put the A-Z down, and reached for a nodule on one of his necks. He gave it a tweak.

"Sorry, mate," said the first mouth. "I forgot to readjust to Earth language, like. Know what I mean?"

"I got you the magazines," Jamie said. "I couldn't get the DVD, sorry, it's in my brother's room. He's OK. He just doesn't understand about you."

"Not many would, like," the alien answered. "That's why I was glad to meet you, mate."

"Good job you crashed in our back garden," Jamie went on. "And good job the dragon had already gone. Else you'd have had to sleep in the shed instead. And it's so cold out there."

"You were cool." The alien gave Jamie four grins.

"What did you do with the escape pod, by the way?" Jamie asked.

In answer, the alien held up a small, plastic ball.

"I used the miniaturisation function. It can't be used for space travel again, like." He held it out in his third hand to Jamie. "I thought you might like it as a goodbye present."

"Ooh, thanks." Jamie took it smilingly. "It'll do to keep my pencil sharpener in. For school."

"I'll be out of your hair by midnight," the alien continued. "The mothership's going to pick me up outside the off licence."

"That's not far." Jamie nodded.

"All I need to do is teleport over there," the alien finished. "And I've got the energy to do that now. Thanks to you."

He popped the last of the custard cream into his third mouth, and his fourth finished the orangeade.

"Your Earth foods are so good."

"Soon be goodbye, then," Jamie said, sadly. He went over to the alien and they put all their arms round each other.

"I'll call again," the alien said. "And maybe bring one of my mates. This is such a cool planet. Even if you do all look kind of strange."

* * * *

Five minutes later, Neil and Jamie's Mum arrived home. And fifteen minutes after that, she had the boys' tea ready.

"Don't forget your guitar lesson," she told Neil.

"I've been practising." Neil pulled a face. "Think I'm getting the hang of it now."

"And what have *you* been up to?" Mum placed a plate of pasta bake before Jamie.

"Oh, he's been out in the garage." The smirk returned to Neil's face. "Visiting the alien."

"Oh, I heard about him." Mum smiled. "Does the alien want some tea, as well, then?" she asked Jamie.

Jamie shook his head.

"No, thank you. He only needs one meal a day."

"He likes the odd biscuit, though," Neil added.

"Now, that'll do," Mum said. "Stop teasing your brother."

"He's going tonight," Jamie said. "I'm going to miss him. I'll be in bed when he leaves."

"Oh, dear." Mum smiled.

"Who's coming next then?" Neil asked, grinning.

"I don't know." Jamie frowned. "I got a call from a magic rabbit… but then I've got the unicorn to fit in. I'll have to think about it."

He took a thoughtful mouthful of pasta.

"That's the trouble, you see. With having so many friends."

The Secret

I've got a secret.

I didn't have, this morning. But I do now.

It's a big secret. One that no one else knows.

It's a secret about Lauren.

I heard it at lunchtime, from Danny. And he swore me to complete secrecy.

So don't say anything.

It's definitely true. Danny heard it straight from James, in his maths group. And James heard it straight from Jessica and Amy. He met them in the yard at break. And Jessica and Amy got it straight from Rebecca, who heard it from Charlotte, who lives in the same road as Sophie, who's Lauren's best friend. So it must be true.

But don't say anything.

I don't spread secrets round, of course. Once you tell me something, it goes no further. You could trust me with anything. I knew about Amy's pierced ears before anyone else, because I heard it from her cousin. I knew who was going to be in the football team for the Churchwood match, long before they put the notice up. And I knew when Miss Boyd was getting married. Well, I was passing the staff room and it's not my fault if they leave the door open. But I didn't tell anyone. No one heard any of it from me.

So say nothing.

Lots of people could have secrets, if you stop to think about it. And no one might ever know about them. You see people going into school every morning, and, from their faces, you might think everything was OK. But you can't really know, can you, everything that goes on in their lives? In their homes, their families? Or anywhere else, apart from school? They could be doing anything, after the bell. Or in the mornings, before school starts. Or at weekends. And, if they didn't tell anyone, or if no one found out, then no one would know. Anyone you meet, in class, or in the yard, or on the playing field, could have a secret.

But I bet no one has a secret quite like Lauren's.

It's something that Lauren wouldn't want anyone to know. She only heard the news herself a few days ago. At first, no one knew outside her house. Her Mum and Dad know, of course. Well, they would, wouldn't they? And her big sister still lives at home, so she knows too. There are just the four of them at home. Plus the dog, of course. But I don't suppose the dog knows. At least, if it does, it probably won't tell anyone.

Don't you say anything to anyone, will you?

Lauren's very excited about it. And she would be, wouldn't she? It's not the sort of thing that happens to everyone. I don't think it's ever happened to anyone in our school before. Or likely to again, for a good long time. Sophie was very excited too. Well, she would be, as Lauren's her best friend. And Charlotte was excited as well, when she heard the news. And Rebecca, even though she doesn't really know Lauren that well. And when she told Jessica and Amy, they were very excited. And James, when he heard about it from them at breaktime. And I suppose Danny was excited, since he told me in the dinner queue. Difficult to tell though, with Danny. He doesn't show his feelings much.

Don't say a word, will you?

I suppose a lot of people will know before very long. After all, it's not the sort of thing that often happens to people, even in a big town like this. That's why everyone was so excited. It could be in the newspapers. The local ones at least. And on the local news. Maybe the TV cameras will come to school. It's time they did. They haven't been since that politician came to visit. You remember, when I represented our year group, and we stood in the hall for two hours waiting for him to arrive, and when he did, he only had time for a quick look at my fantastic article that went up on the wall, before he shot off again to visit somewhere else. And then the story got cut, and I didn't even get to be on the telly.

This is at least as important as that. And so Lauren could be on the telly. And if the cameras and reporters do come to school, maybe we can be on the telly too. And everyone will know that we're Lauren's friends. Or if we're not, then it's time we started. Before long, everyone could know Lauren's secret.

But the point of a secret is that it should stay a

secret. Isn't it? It should be a secret until Lauren wants everyone to know. That's why she only told Sophie. And why Sophie only told Charlotte. And why Charlotte only told Rebecca. And why Rebecca only told Jessica and Amy, and…well, you know the rest.

So don't say I said anything, will you?

I'd love to do what Lauren's going to do. It'll be so good. More fun than anything that happens around here. I don't do anything like that. I just do the football team and the Scrabble club. And that's not what it was, since they moved it to after school on Thursdays. And outside school, I've got trumpet, and judo. And that's it.

Lauren's going to have some real fun. She could be famous, before long. We could all be asking for her autograph. And she'll be earning money as well. Far more than I'll ever earn. And she'll get to know some really cool people.

But she'll still have to pass her exams.

I hope it doesn't change her too much.

Don't tell anyone I spoke to you, will you?

Well, that's it. That's my bus stop. I'd better go. Got homework to do. I haven't got far to walk, just to the end of the road, and then…

Oh, what d'you say? Sorry?

I haven't told you what it is yet? What what is?

Oh, the secret?

Lauren's secret?

You want to know what the secret is?

Sorry…afraid I can't tell you that.

It's a secret.

The Battle of the Bulge

Juniper Class all saw it, that Tuesday morning.

It wasn't something they were likely to have missed.

Liam, the tallest member of the class, saw it straight away. So did Justin, his sidekick. And the rest of Liam's gang. Kimberley noticed it too. And her friend, Sophie. And some of the other girls.

In Nicholas Phelps's schoolbag, a mysterious object had appeared.

Normally, most of them hardly looked at Nicholas. He never went round with Liam's gang. They never asked him. He was the quiet one of the class. He always did his homework on time. He never got detention. He was polite to all the teachers. And his schoolbag was always neatly packed, the books and pencil case tidily slotted in.

But today, a new, strange item had appeared. Almost too much for the bag to hold, when packed in with everything else.

On one side of the bag, as it rested there on his skinny shoulders, something unknown was bulging out, for all to see.

The other members of the class were only slightly interested, at first.

"What you got in there?" Liam demanded, as they lined up in the yard before Assembly.

"Pardon?" Nicholas, in his usual place at the front

of the line, turned to look up at the tall, blond boy.

"There!" Liam pointed. "In your bag."

"Oh." Nicholas didn't sound at all interested. "Nothing."

Standing behind Liam, Justin shuffled forward to join his leader. He was a stocky, tanned boy.

"Don't look like nothing," he observed. He reached out a finger and poked the bulge. "What is it?"

"Hey, get off!" Nicholas pulled away. He looked at Liam, slightly uneasily. "It's nothing, really. Nothing much, anyway. Just…something I need."

Liam looked at Nicholas, rather like a fox might look at a particularly timid rabbit.

If Liam wanted to know what was in the bag, Nicholas would tell him…

But at that moment, the teachers appeared to bring them inside, and Nicholas was saved.

As he moved off, Liam and Justin took another curious look at the mystery object that Nicholas had brought to school. What could it be?

Other members of the class had seen it too.

"What d'you reckon it is?" Liam wondered. He and his gang were sitting round one of the tables in their classroom, half-heartedly doing Maths. He looked at Justin. "Not like him to bring anything special to school. What did it feel like?"

"I dunno." Justin shrugged. "Soft. That's all, really."

"Could be something someone gave him." Ben, Liam's third-in-command, spoke. He was a thin, sharp-featured boy. On first sighting it looked as if a rat had somehow found its way into a school uniform. "Birthday present or something. People sometimes bring stuff in…"

"It's not his birthday." Liam provided leadership. "His birthday's in April. I remember 'cause it was just after my sister's."

"Wait 'til break." Justin clenched a fist. He liked to think of himself as the tough guy of the class, the muscles of Liam's gang. "I'll ask him again."

"Nah." Liam looked thoughtful. "I know Nick. You won't get at him that way. No, you've got to be a bit clever."

Justin looked disappointed.

Liam leaned in closer, and his gang followed him. He lowered his voice.

"Here's what we do."

Across the classroom, around another table, the girls were having a similar conversation.

"I don't know what it is," Sophie was saying. "Bet Liam finds out."

"Him?" Kimberley curled her lip. She was a big, rather bossy girl. If there was a secret to be found out, Kimberley was going to find it first. "He couldn't find out that today's Wednesday."

"It's Tuesday actually," Emily, the most timid member of Kimberley's band, put in quietly.

Kimberley ignored her.

"I want to find out." When Kimberley said she

wanted something, there were no arguments. She smiled slightly. "Think I know how."

Break came.

Juniper Class, along with everyone else, filed out into the yard.

Break time was normally a time Nicholas hated. He would either be standing in a corner on his own, or surrounded by the other kids, Liam's gang especially, who would take the mickey out of him.

For some reason, today things seemed to be different. As soon as he went outside, there were Liam and his mates. But they seemed oddly friendly.

"You all right, Nick?" Liam gave Nicholas a grin, which was rather scarier than his usual look. "Come round with us?"

Nicholas allowed himself to be led away to the playing field, where Liam and co. usually met.

"Like a crisp?" Justin never liked delays on the food. He ripped open the bag and held it out to Nicholas. "New kind. Roast beef and parsnip flavour. They're dead nice."

"Oh." Uncertainly, Nicholas took one. "Thank you."

"Have some chocolate, too." Ben shared his own snack with the newest member of the gang.

They stood on the rough grass in silence for a moment or so.

"We were wondering what was in your bag," Justin said abruptly. "Aaargghh!"

He grabbed his ankle at a sudden pain.

"Oh!" Liam smiled angelically, and moved his foot. "Sorry." He addressed Nicholas. "Don't listen to him. He's a professional idiot. We just thought we'd like to talk to you. No sense, you always standing there on your own."

"It's nothing anyway," Nicholas put in. "Nothing interesting."

"'Course not," Liam agreed. He gave Justin a look that said: *You're dead.*

There was another awkward silence.

Eventually Liam spoke again.

"Hey Nick…I'm…having a few mates round to mine, after school. You can…come along, if you like."

"Oh." Nicholas shrugged. "Thanks."

"And bring your schoolbag," Justin finished. "Ow!"

He doubled up in pain, at another correction from his leader.

Over by the hopscotch grid, an argument was taking place.

"I don't see why it has to be me!" Emily was saying wildly.

"He likes you," Kimberley said firmly. "You get on with him."

"I don't even know him that well!" poor Emily protested.

"You're the only one." Sophie stuck up for her leader, as ever. "He's not going to fancy Kimberley, is he?"

Kimberley shot her a look.

"But on a date!" Emily cried.

"Not a date exactly," Kimberley said. "Just invite

him over to yours, for tea. Today."

"I've got Guides tonight!" Emily objected.

"All right then," Kimberley said. "Tomorrow. Get him to yours, straight from school. Then all you've got to do is find the moment…and search his bag."

Kimberley sniffed.

"Teach him to be so secretive."

Emily looked dumbfounded.

Not for the first time, she was starting to think Kimberley was just a bit mad.

Nicholas suddenly seemed to be popular everywhere. After school, everyone stared in amazement at the sight of him leaving at the centre of Liam's gang, in pride of place. Very few boys made it there.

The stories went around the school quickly, as they always did. Nicholas had been round to Liam's, with the rest of the gang, for pizza. He'd been invited to Liam's birthday party, at World of Go-Cart. And the next morning, another story was round the Breakfast Club before you could say "toast".

Emily Jarvis had asked Nicholas on a date.

Or at least, for tea.

"And remember," Kimberley said to her firmly. "We're relying on you."

Emily was nervous.

Nicholas would be arriving at any moment.

And she was desperately hoping he wouldn't come.

She stood in the narrow hallway of her home,

looking at her watch. Normally, it would have been fun, having someone round for tea. She'd always quite liked Nicholas. He was one of the quieter ones in the class, like her. She'd found some board games for them to play. And Mum was in the kitchen, cooking them fish fingers and chips. Yes, this should have been fun.

But it wasn't going to be fun for Emily. Because Emily had a mission to fulfil. Somehow, at some point during the evening, she had to get Nicholas out of the way and search his schoolbag for the mysterious object. And Emily had no idea how she was going to do it.

She'd tried and tried to think out a plan. But she wasn't Kimberley, and nothing had come.

She shot out of her skin as the doorbell rang.

That was him.

She paused for a moment. Took a deep breath. Then she stepped forward and opened the door.

She stopped and stared. Then a wonderful feeling of relief spread through her.

Nicholas stood there. In ordinary clothes. Dark trousers, and a rather awful plaid shirt. And there was no sign of his schoolbag.

"Sorry I'm late," he said, with his usual politeness. "I stopped off at home to change. Dump my stuff."

Emily could have hugged him, but she settled for a smile.

"That's cool. Come on in."

And Nicholas came in.

Emily's smile was getting bigger and bigger. This was going to be a fun evening, after all.

The next morning was not quite so fun.

Kimberley and Sophie stood on the netball court with Emily, looking like the Ugly Sisters confronting Cinderella.

"I knew it!" Kimberley was saying furiously. "I knew you'd mess it up."

"It's not her fault he didn't bring his bag," Sophie ventured.

Kimberley incinerated her with a glance.

"Now that boy Liam's going to find out first!" She made the discovery of what was in Nicholas's bag sound as important as a bid for the Olympics. She paused. "We'll have to think of something else."

"Oh, well…" Emily started to move away.

Kimberley stared at her, like a general finding half his army had gone off for tea.

"Where are you going?"

"Talk to Nicholas." Emily gave Kimberley a big smile. "I'd love to stop and talk, but…" She turned away from the bigger girls. "See you."

Kimberley stared, dumbfounded, as Emily walked away and left her standing there.

Sophie stifled a smile.

Most of the class went to Liam's party.

Nicholas sat on a bench, enjoying a hot dog amidst the noise and frenzied activity of World of Go-Cart.

On the go-cart track, Justin had somehow managed to crash his car into Kimberley's, and a furious row was going on.

Watching the scene, sitting next to Nicholas, Emily smiled slightly.

She turned to him.

"I enjoyed the other night," she said quietly.

"Yes." Nicholas gave her a brief smile. "Me too."

Liam came over and sat down next to them, taking a break from driving. The birthday boy had sweat on his brow and ketchup round his mouth. He was looking a bit cross.

"I still think Justin had right of way!" He looked at his classmates. "Having fun?"

Kimberley came storming over to them.

"I don't care what he says, that Justin was driving straight at me!" She glared at Liam. "We're meant to be on go-carts, not dodgems!"

She grabbed Emily by the arm.

"Come on. We need to sort this out!"

Helplessly, Emily allowed herself to be led away towards the track.

Liam grinned. He shuffled closer to Nicholas. He paused, rather awkwardly.

"Nick…" he said slowly.

"Mm?" Nicholas looked at him innocently.

"That thing," Liam went on. "In your bag."

"I told you!" Nicholas insisted. "It's nothing!"

"No!" Liam replied hastily. "I know. 'Course not. But…" He hesitated. "You will let us see it. Sometime. Won't you?"

Nicholas was silent for a moment. Then he shrugged.

"OK. If you really want to. It's not much though, really."

Liam looked delighted – and quite relieved.

"Cool!"

He got up and paused to slap Nicholas on the back, nearly sending him onto the floor.

"See you later then, mate. Glad you could make it."

He swaggered off, to join his friends. There was a look of triumph on his face.

Nicholas sat a little longer, watching the track. Contentedly, he finished off the hot dog.

It was Monday evening. Almost a week since Nicholas had first brought the mystery object to school.

Nicholas stepped into his bedroom and closed the door. He swung his schoolbag down from his shoulder, and placed it on the floor.

He started to unpack it.

It had been a good day at school. One of his best ever. Liam and the gang had let him right to the front of the queue for lunch in the canteen. Kimberley and Sophie had presented him with a slightly awful collage they'd made in Art. And Emily was coming for tea with him tomorrow night. He was getting on very well with her.

The bulging object in his schoolbag had turned out to be very useful. Everyone now wanted to know what it was.

Smiling slightly, he reached into the bag, found the mystery item, and pulled it out.

The spare pair of socks Mum had given him for PE.

Homework

"Why would you do that, anyway?" Justin asked.

"Huh?" Liam looked up from his Maths book.

"Have a bag full of counters." Justin looked at his worksheet. He was two questions behind Liam. "Look…you've got this bag, with eight red counters in, four blue ones and eight green ones. And someone's gonna take two of 'em out…I mean, why would you do that? What's it for?"

"Just Maths, innit?" Liam shrugged. "It's not real life."

"Probability." Justin returned to his work. "Weird."

The two of them were lying sprawled out on the living room carpet, round at Liam's house. Liam's elder sister was upstairs, getting ready for a night out. From time to time, they heard the bang of the bathroom door, and the creak of floorboards as she moved about in her room above them. Otherwise, everything was peaceful.

"Wish I was better at Maths." Justin had smudged the ink from his biro across his answers to questions 8 and 9. He rubbed at the smudge carelessly with his thumb. He looked at his friend. "Would you like to be good at Maths, Liam?"

"What d'you mean?" Liam looked insulted. "I *am* good at Maths! I come fourth in the Friday test – *every* week!"

"Naah." Justin wrote number 11 in his book and drew a circle round it, slowly, thoughtfully. "I mean, *really* good at Maths. Like that…what's-her-name. Thingie. Off the telly. Her off *Countdown*."

"Oh." Liam was trying to do question 13 on the calculator on his mobile. "Dunno. I suppose being famous would be nice. You're famous if you're on TV."

"I wouldn't mind being famous." Justin scratched his nose with the end of his pen. "Have your photo in magazines. Get to wear all those really cool clothes." He reached inside the collar of his baggy tracksuit top and had another scratch. "Go on those reality shows…"

"Reality TV?" Liam had given up on the calculation and was texting their friend Ben. "Going in the jungle? Eating earwigs? No thank you!"

"I wonder what earwigs taste like?" Justin reached out a hand and slid another chocolate digestive from the blue-rimmed plate that lay on the floor by them. He took half of the biscuit into his mouth with one bite. "Bet I could eat them."

"You probably would an' all." Liam sent his message and returned, reluctantly, to question 13.

There was a moment's silence, during which Justin finished his biscuit and reached for his can of Coke. Liam had an empty Tango can at his elbow.

"No," Liam went on. "Don't bother with reality TV. Thing to do, if you're a lad and want to be famous. Be a professional footballer. Then you've got loads of cash. And everyone thinks you're cool."

"Like Courtney Westbrook." Justin moved onto question 12.

"What?" Liam looked up from number 14.

"Courtney Westbrook," Justin repeated.

"Courtney Westbrook!" Liam had a good go at sniggering and sneering at the same time.

"He's a good footballer," Justin protested.

"You telling me he's your idea of a great footballer?" Liam scoffed. "Him from Oak Class? With that mad haircut, and football stickers all over his bag? The boy who landed our football on the roof? Him? He's not a footballer!"

There was a pause.

"Well, he beat you," Justin said eventually.

"You *what*?" Liam spluttered.

"Well, your team." Justin put his pen down. "Our team. When we played Oak Class. Five-a-side. Six-one, the score, wasn't it?"

"I always said Ben was rubbish in goal." Liam suddenly seemed to be very busy on question 14. "I'm a brilliant centre forward. That Courtney Westbrook…" He made a scornful sound.

After a moment, Justin returned also to Probability.

"What number are you on?" he asked.

"Fourteen," Liam said shortly.

"I'm catching you up." Justin grinned. "I'm on thirteen now." He looked at the worksheet again and frowned. "How many cards in a pack?"

"Fifty-two." Liam was having another go at the mobile's calculator. "Cloth-head."

"There's only forty-seven in ours." Justin took a swig from the Coke can. "Like when my brother showed me how to play poker. I knew he was cheating when he said he'd got four Aces. We ain't *got* four Aces."

He looked down at his book once more.

There was another silence.

"Kimberley's having a party," Justin said finally.

Liam lost count on question 15 and looked up. "What?"

"Sophie told me," Justin went on. "Next Saturday. At Spoil 'Em Rotten. You know, that place where they go to be…what d'you call it…pampered."

"Eeughh." Liam pulled a face.

"What they do is," Justin explained, "they get 'em all there, and they give 'em a makeover. They do stuff to their eyes, and their lips, and put make-up on…all that stuff." He was making signs to illustrate this, like cabin crew giving a safety talk. "And then, they put stuff on their nails, which is all sort of sparkly so they -"

"Have you been to this place?" Liam lost count again and his temper with it.

"No…" Justin answered.

"D'you want to?" Liam demanded.

"No…"

"Well, shut up, then!"

There was another silence, rather longer this time.

Then both of them returned quietly to their work.

Forty-seven seconds later, Liam said:

"Sorry."

"No worries." Justin had been down this road with Liam many times. He gave his friend a grin before returning to drawing a star around the figure 14 in his book.

There was another long pause.

"Suppose the world was ending," Justin said suddenly.

"You what?" Liam looked baffled.

"Say the world," Justin said, "was coming to an end. You were the last guy left alive. There was only one girl left alive. And you could choose what girl. Who'd it be?"

Liam gave the question some thought.

"That girl off T4," he said finally.

"Oh, her," Justin agreed. "Yeah, she's all right."

"Yeah…" said Liam thoughtfully. "The T4 girl." He paused. "Or Sharon Gunning. From Heather Class."

Having settled this, he returned to Probability.

Another silence followed.

Justin stared at his worksheet for a moment, then looked at Liam.

"What've you got for fourteen?" he demanded. He leaned over to Liam's exercise book and prodded the page Liam was working on. "See, here, I got…"

"Hey!" Liam gave a cry as Justin's chubby finger appeared in the middle of number 14. "You twit! Look what you've done!"

As Justin's finger moved away, a smeary chocolaty

smudge was left across Liam's calculations on several people tossing a coin.

"Look at that!" Liam spluttered. "How can I hand that in to Jenkins? Probability four over splodge!"

"Flip." Justin rubbed his hands on his sleeves. "Sorry, mate."

"Well, I'm not writing it out again!" Liam grabbed his pencil case from the rug. "Where's the Tipp-Ex?"

There was another interval while he tried to repair the damage.

Finally, he said to Justin:

"Four over sixteen. Or a quarter."

"Ta." Justin wrote it in.

Another pause.

"I'm on nineteen now," Liam said presently. "Just finished eighteen."

"I'm still on sixteen," Justin said. He pulled a face. "Ah, let's speed it up. What've you got? Sixteen to eighteen?"

"OK." Liam read from his book. "Sixteen is three over four."

"Three over four." Justin wrote it quickly in his own book.

"Seventeen is eight," Liam continued.

"Eight." Justin scribbled it down.

"And eighteen is a carrot."

"A carrot." Justin had actually written the words in his book before he realised. He looked up to see Liam grinning broadly. "Oh, very funny."

"Gotcha!" Liam crowed. He made the sign of someone chalking up one-all on a board.

He returned to number 19, while Justin reached for the Tipp-Ex. Once again, there was a moment's silence.

"Why do they call it Heather Class?" Justin said, once the Tipp-Ex was drying over "A carrot".

"What?" Liam had reached 19 b).

"Well, heather's a bush." Justin poked the patch of Tipp-Ex to see if it was dry. "I saw it on holiday. In Scotland. All the other classes are trees. Cedar, Oak, we're Juniper…"

"Teachers' names, innit?" Liam explained. "First letters. Cedar is Mrs Charles, Oak's Mr Oliver, we've got Jenkins…Heather's Mrs Hoyle…"

"And heather's a bush," Justin insisted. "Isn't it?"

"Oh yeah." Liam thought for a moment. "There's another H, Mrs Hoskins…Guess they ran out of trees starting with H."

"S'pose." Justin probed the Tipp-Ex again. "Hmm." He wrote the correct answer in.

Another pause.

"There we go!" Liam finished number 20, folded his worksheet and closed his book with a smirk. "Finished."

"Aw!" Justin whined. "I'm still only on nineteen a)!"

"Your fault." Smugly, Liam flipped himself over and lay on the carpet, stretching out his long legs. "Shouldn't have talked so much, should you? Take an example from your leader."

He let Justin look fed up for just so long.

"Go on. Copy the others off me."

"Oh, cheers!" Justin grabbed Liam's book and copied the last few answers. "There we go. Brilliant."

They got up from the carpet.

"What shall we do now?" Liam asked. "TV? Wii?"

"I reckon Wii," Justin said. "See if I can beat you this time."

The two of them shoved their books into their bags and headed for the door.

"There's one thing," Justin said, as they made for Liam's room. "No one can say we don't do our work."

Remote Control

Dominic was crying again.

Amy stuck her fingers in her ears, trying in vain to block out the sound. Her brother was nearly two now. Shouldn't little kids be talking by that age? Burbling, anyway. Saying: "Mama!" or something. Not sitting there, screaming their heads off.

If Dad had been there, he could have kept Dominic quiet. Amy was sure of that.

She looked, as she often did, towards the family portrait on the wall. Mum had left it there so as not to upset her. The large framed photograph had been taken the Christmas before last. There they all were, Mum, holding a tiny Dominic proudly in her arms, then Amy herself, a little younger, then Dad, grinning for the camera, the proud father of two children.

Five months after that photograph had been taken, Dad had left. Amy only saw him at weekends now.

And four months after that, Louis had come on the scene.

Dominic's howls were getting louder, and Amy couldn't take it any more.

"Mum!" She had to bellow to be heard above the bawling toddler.

"What?" Mum yelled back, from the kitchen.

"Dominic's crying again!"

"I can't come now!" Mum's voice sounded distant. Where's she shouting from, Amy wondered? Like, France? "He's teething! You can take care of him, can't you, sweetheart? Be a love!"

Amy groaned to herself. Why was she always expected to be a love? No one else round here ever was.

She looked at Dominic. What was she meant to do? Go over and hug him? He had raspberry jam all round his mouth. And felt tip on his yellow Bunnykin jumper. And his chestnut brown hair was all over the place, just like…

Just like Dad's had been. First thing in the morning.

That was another reason why she didn't like Dominic.

She certainly wasn't doing any hugging. Pursing her lips, she turned back to the TV and tried to hear the latest episode of *Angst*.

It wasn't fair. She'd have homework to do later, and the one half-hour she had to watch her favourite soap before tea, Dominic had to ruin for her. It wasn't as if tea itself would be any good.

"She's eating all the wrong stuff," Louis had said, in front of her, shortly after his arrival. And that had been the start of an endless round of salads, and tofu, and oily fish, and yoghurt.

She hadn't minded Mum joining a gym. She might not even have minded Mum finding a new boyfriend. But why had Mum had to bring the one home from the other?

If Amy ever fell in love, it was not going to be with a Fitness Instructor.

She couldn't hear this programme! She made a lunge for the coffee table, and seized the remote control.

It was a large, black, shiny remote control, with big buttons, some in different colours for the interactive functions. It controlled the widescreen TV, video recorder and the Sky box.

"Integration," Louis had said, on bringing a lot of this stuff into the house in the first place. "Everything in one. That's the way ahead."

Of course, Louis knew everything.

Amy pressed the Volume control, trying to turn the TV up. Nothing was happening. Useless. Just like the guy who'd bought it. She pressed and pressed the little Plus symbol, but the sound stayed low. Oh!

She glared at Dominic. The TV would be quite loud enough, if he would just be quiet. It didn't really need turning up at all.

She wished she could turn him down instead.

Idly, she pretended to do just that, pointing the remote at her brother and pressing the Minus symbol on the Volume button.

A moment later, she almost dropped the remote in shock.

All at once, Dominic was quieter.

It couldn't be. It was just wishful thinking. She had wanted it to happen, and for a second, she had thought it had…

Almost in a trance, Amy raised the remote again,

pointed it at the little boy, and pressed the Minus symbol again.

And a moment later, Dominic was silent.

He didn't seem bothered, but went on playing with the K, T and S bricks that were all that was left of his alphabet set.

Amy felt a sudden, wonderful surge of excitement.

She pressed the Plus. Dominic's voice rose again. She pressed Minus. Once more, he was silent.

She pointed the remote at the TV, pressed Plus, Minus and several of the channel controls. Nothing was happening there.

Did it work on other things, besides Dominic?

She had to find out.

"Amy!" Mum's voice came. Quickly, Amy raised the remote and pointed it towards the kitchen. She pressed Plus.

When the second "Amy!" came a moment later, it nearly deafened her. She pressed Minus.

"Amy?" Mum paused. She sounded taken aback by the volume of her own voice. "Your tea's ready!"

Amy pulled a face. But she was really excited now. She darted for the sofa, and hid the remote under a cushion, pushing it right to the back. She wasn't having Dominic get his little jammy hands on it. Or anyone, until she'd found out just what else it could do...

There were lots of possibilities...

Amy ran into the kitchen.

"Dominic all right?" Mum turned from the cooker. She had been to the hairdresser's that day, and had the blonde highlights put in. Louis liked her hair that way.

"Yeah," Amy answered. She grinned brightly. "I quietened him down."

Halfway through Amy's veggieburgers, Louis came home. Mum went out to greet him. Amy stayed in the kitchen, thinking about the remote.

There were all kinds of buttons on it. Suppose they all did different things?

She bolted the second half of the meal, and ran back to the living room.

Noooo!

Louis stood there, in his tracksuit and trainers, the remote in his hand.

His thin, sharp-featured face, with its stubbly goatee beard, wore a puzzled frown. He was stabbing the buttons on the remote with his finger, trying to change channels.

"It's not working," was all he said to Amy.

Amy said nothing.

Louis tried his chosen button once more, then gave up.

"Must be the batteries." To Amy's relief, he put the remote down on the coffee table. "I'll have to get some."

Amy watched his tall, lean figure as he moved over to the TV and changed the children's channel to a sports one. She stood for a moment, looking at the back of his shaven head.

What did Mum see in him? Dad had been chubby, easy-going, good-natured. Louis was like a professional footballer, but without the money.

Having found the channel he wanted, Louis bent down and scooped up Dominic from the carpet.

"And how's my little fella?" Grinning, Louis enveloped the toddler in his sinewy arms. Dominic giggled. "Eh? Eh?"

His little fella? Amy felt the veggieburgers coming back.

Holding Dominic firmly, Louis sat down in Dad's corner chair, the one with the best view of the TV. Still ignoring Amy, he spoke again to the toddler.

"Gonna watch the footie, aren't we? Eh?"

Amy sat on the sofa, her eyes flaming.

"Haven't you got homework?" Louis didn't look away from the screen as he asked Amy that question.

Oh, thought Amy. I am so going to get you.

Suddenly, she thought of the remote.

Very quietly, she reached out to the table and lifted it. Louis didn't notice. Very slowly, she turned it so that it pointed directly at him.

What should she press? There were so many buttons to try…

A smile spread slowly across her face. Moving her finger away from the TV controls, she reached instead for the video buttons. Her finger settled on the one with the symbol that always looked, to Amy, like a little house. The button for Eject…

With a yell, Louis seemed to take a flying leap out of his chair. He almost dropped Dominic, but managed to grab hold of him.

He looked round, wondered what on earth had

happened. Amy bit her lip, desperately trying to hold back laughter. Louis had looked silly, and that was something he did not like.

"You all right?" Amy asked sweetly.

"Oh. Yeah…" Louis looked nonplussed, and Amy was going redder and redder. "Bit of cramp." He put Dominic down carefully in the chair. "Happens, of course." He rubbed his ankle thoughtfully.

"Too much exercise," Amy suggested.

Louis ignored this.

"Think I'll go and have a hot bath." He headed for the door.

Amy grinned. Her head was full of ideas now. Keeping the remote in her lap, she turned it towards Louis again as he moved across the room, and pressed Stop.

Louis froze. He didn't just stop walking. Everything about him stood still, arms, hands, face. He was like a statue.

Amy couldn't keep silent any more. She shrieked with laughter. She pressed Play. Louis started to move forward again. She pressed Stop. He skidded to a halt again, and almost fell, before freezing. Unable to resist, Amy pressed Play again. Louis toppled over and lay in a heap.

Amy buried her face in the cushion she had used earlier.

"Louis?" Mum came dashing in, much to Amy's disgust. "Louis? You all right, babe? What happened?"

"I fell." Slightly shakily, Louis got up. "Think I'm OK. Touch of cramp."

"Oh!" Mum put her arms round him and hugged him. Reluctantly, Amy decided not to risk being seen pressing any other button. "Come on, I'll run you a bath. Then I'll cook something for both of us…"

She turned coldly as Amy let another snigger slip out.

"Shouldn't you be doing homework?"

"Just going." Amy got up, a smirk on her face. She was pleased to see Mum looking annoyed and puzzled. She reached for her schoolbag, which lay on the floor by the sofa. The remote control was still in her hand. Unseen by Mum, who was fussing over Louis, Amy slipped the remote quietly into her bag.

All that evening, Amy was buzzing at the thought of her new toy. There were so many things she could do…

She was expecting to be challenged at any minute, for Mum, or Louis, to ask where the remote was. But neither of them said anything to her about it.

It was still in her bag when she set off for school the next morning. Her excitement had kept her awake for some time, and as a result she had slept late and had to be woken by Mum. Most of Holly Class were already gathered in the playground by the time she arrived.

Amy looked for Jessica, her best friend, but Jessica was standing with some of the other girls, listening to Georgia. Georgia had a new coat on, with the usual designer label, and her hair looked fabulous. Nearby,

Rachel Nelson was standing, a tubby figure in a much older coat, trying not to be seen.

Georgia had just said something, and all the girls were laughing – all except Rachel, who was looking at the ground.

It wasn't fair, Amy thought. The way they picked on Rachel. Of course, everyone thought Georgia was great. Georgia's Dad was rich. Georgia had been to California for her holidays. When the TV crew had been to school, the teachers had chosen Georgia to talk to them about the class's environmental project. And Georgia had made it sound as though she had done the whole thing.

Narrowing her eyes, Amy started to open her schoolbag.

The bell rang.

"Come on now!" Mrs Hoskins had come out of the school building, looking hassled. "Into line! That means you, Elliott!"

The girls started to move into line.

Then, all at once, Georgia was no longer with them.

She was moving backwards.

And not walking, but running.

There were gasps, and then giggling, as Georgia, Head of Blue Team and Dance Club Champion, sped backwards towards the school gate.

"Georgia!" Mrs Hoskins bellowed. "Georgia! Come back here at once!"

The only answer was a scream from Georgia as she disappeared from view.

No one was looking at Amy. Quietly, she removed her finger from the Rewind button, and slipped the remote back into her bag.

Georgia was rather quieter than usual when she reappeared in school. As she entered the classroom for Communal Act of Worship, she avoided Mrs Hoskins' eye.

Afterwards, they did Maths. Amy was still thinking about Rachel. It wasn't fair that she should be picked on. It wasn't fair that Georgia was certainly the prettiest girl in the class.

If only Rachel could be that pretty. Amy looked at Rachel's mousy hair and pasty skin. Georgia's hair shone, and she had a lovely tan. If Rachel had a tan, she would look better…

Then Amy had an idea. Pretending to need a pencil sharpener, she reached down to her schoolbag for her pencil box, then, with a lightning movement, brought out the remote control as well and shoved it into the pocket of her cardigan. Now, with a little care, she could aim the remote at Rachel without it being seen.

Amy reached deeper into her pocket. The night before, in her room, she had really studied the remote, and she now knew where all the buttons were without looking. The button she wanted was for adjusting the Colour on the TV…

She pressed it. For a second, nothing seemed to happen to Rachel, and it looked as though her plan had failed. Then she blinked.

Rachel's skin was changing. Darkening. She already looked as though she had been on holiday for a week. A moment later, her tan was as good as Georgia's.

Amy let go of the button, and smiled to herself.

Her new toy was useful for helping people too.

No one remarked on Rachel's tan until break, when she suddenly found herself the centre of attention.

"That is *so* good!" Ignoring Georgia now, Jessica linked her left arm with Rachel's and offered the right arm to Amy. "You look wicked! Is it Body Lotion or real thing?"

"I…" Rachel seemed more surprised and pleased than anyone. "I didn't use anything. Must have just been in the sun."

"Well, it's cool anyway," Jessica said. "Isn't it, Amy?"

"You look great." Amy smiled.

"Weird how we didn't see it this morning," Jessica mused. She turned back to Rachel. "Are you coming to my party on Friday then?"

Amy did a few other good deeds during the day, unknown to anyone else. When Liam and Justin's football ended up on the roof at afternoon break, a quick press on the Eject button brought it springing down. She helped one of the smallest Infants do incredibly well in a game of hopscotch, using the channel-hopping button. And the old Reveal button from Teletext gave Holly Class a laugh in the final lesson, when Mrs Hoskins' blouse suddenly became rather transparent.

"That's gross," Jermaine Barnes was heard to mutter.

There was no homework that night, and after school Amy went home with Jessica, and Rachel came too, and they stayed for tea. And there were chips, much to Amy's delight. Afterwards, the Nintendo kept them busy until it was time for Amy to head home.

For a short time, she had almost forgotten about the remote.

"Shut up."

Amy muttered the words to Dominic, as they sat in front of the TV. It was too late for him, wasn't it? Why wasn't he in bed?

Dominic's whining grew louder.

"I said shut up." Amy wanted to finish the programme she was watching, and once again, she couldn't hear a thing.

That little pain in the bum was so asking for it…

Dominic's mouth opened wide, and a howl emerged that seemed to split Amy's eardrums.

"I said shut up!"

Grabbing the remote from the table, Amy aimed it at her little brother. She wanted something more than reduced Volume this time. Without hesitating for a second, she hit Mute.

Instantly, Dominic was silent.

Amy leaned back on the sofa with a smirk. That had shut him up.

"Amy!"

Amy turned as Mum and Louis entered the room.

Louis had worked late that evening, taking an Aerobics class, and Mum had cooked them both a meal on his return.

"Time you were in bed," Mum said to Amy shortly.

"What about him?" Amy pointed to the silent toddler.

"Him too," Mum admitted. She moved across to Dominic.

"Oh, there it is!"

Before Amy knew what was happening, Louis's hand came down and plucked the remote from her grasp.

"I was looking for that." Louis's fingers moved to the back of the remote, removing the lid from the battery chamber. "Got some new batteries." He pulled out the existing batteries.

"No, hang on -" Amy started to protest. She had to un-silence Dominic!

"Amy!" Mum frowned. "I said bed."

There was nothing that Amy could do. She left the room, able only to glance back at Dominic, still silent as Mum picked him up, and at her precious remote, in the hands of Louis.

With a slightly worried look on her face, Amy went upstairs.

Once in bed, lying in the darkness, Amy thought quickly.

It was all right. Louis would just change the batteries and then put the remote back on the table or TV. After that, it would soon be hers again. She could easily give Dominic his voice back in the morning.

Reassured, she went to sleep.

She wasn't sure what time it was at first when she next woke. But she knew it wasn't time to get up. Everywhere was still dark. Though there was light, a distant light…

The cobwebs of sleep started to clear. The light was on in Mum and Dad's room.

Mum and Louis's room.

And in Dominic's room.

She looked at the clock. It was 3am!

She could hear voices. Distant voices, coming closer. Louis's voice, sounding fed up and tired. And Mum's, high-pitched, anxious.

"Call the doctor, then," Louis was saying.

"Forget the doctor!" Mum cried. "I'm calling 999!"

"And telling 'em what?" Louis demanded. "That the little brat's quiet for once?"

"Don't you talk about my son like that!" Mum's voice came back. "There's something wrong, I know there is! If you don't care, maybe I'll call someone who does!"

"No, look!" Louis sounded more reasonable now. "Wait a sec!"

The voices passed Amy's room. A moment later, she heard both of them disappearing downstairs.

What was -? What had Mum said?

Her son…

Dominic!

She leapt out of bed, ran onto the landing and pushed open wide the door of Dominic's room.

As the door opened, Dominic sat up in his cot and smiled at her. A moment later, his mouth was moving. He was trying to make sounds. But none were coming.

She darted back to her own room as she heard Mum and Louis coming back upstairs.

"It must be his throat!" Mum was saying. "I've never known him so quiet! It's his throat! Maybe he's got breathing difficulties!"

"You'd know if he'd got breathing difficulties!" Louis told her.

"Mum?" Pretending just to have got up, Amy opened her bedroom door. "What's wrong?"

There was a moment's silence.

"Your Mum thinks there's something up with Dominic," Louis said eventually.

"Oh, "thinks"!" Mum glared at him. "Thanks very much! Maybe you'll think I'm still making it up if Dominic never makes a sound again!"

She headed for their bedroom.

"I'm going to get dressed and I'm going in the ambulance with Dom. You can stay here and look after Amy!"

Thanks, Amy thought.

She could see that Louis, now that he had woken up and his bad mood had passed, was just as worried as Mum. As Mum disappeared, he moved into Dominic's room and stood looking at the silent little boy.

Amy ran for the stairs.

She had to give Dom his voice back before the ambulance got there!

Once in the living room, she switched on the light. Where was the remote? It didn't seem to be anywhere! She looked on the coffee table, on the mantelpiece, on top of the TV… It wasn't there! What had Louis done with it?

Finally she found it, in the kitchen, on top of the fridge. Of all places! That idiot Louis must have changed the batteries in the kitchen and left it there.

She had only a little time to spare.

Mum, now hastily dressed, was carrying an equally hastily dressed Dominic downstairs. Louis was following.

Amy dodged out of sight, behind the living room door. She had to get a clear shot at Dominic, without Mum or Louis seeing.

What did you press, to put the sound back? Mute again, wasn't it? Quickly, she moved her finger to the button, and pressed.

Out in the hall, Dominic's mouth moved. But still he was silent.

Frantically, Amy pressed again, and again. And still no sound came from her brother.

What was wrong?

The batteries! It was the batteries! Louis had put new ones in! Whatever power the remote had had, must have come from the old ones.

What had Louis done with them?

"I'm going to keep a look out!" Mum opened the front door, and stood watching for the ambulance.

"Louis!" Amy ran out of the living room. "Where did you put the batteries?"

"You what?" Louis stared at her.

"The batteries!" Amy cried. "The ones you took out of the remote! Where are they?"

"In the kitchen bin," Louis answered. "But -?"

But Amy had disappeared. The kitchen bin!

The kitchen bin was a tall, white, plastic one, and she had to go into the cupboard under the sink to get to it. It was grimy round there, and gungy, and when she opened the bin the smell was foul. The rubbish inside was tied up in a plastic bag, and she found herself fighting with one of Mum's horrible knots to get it open.

"Here's the ambulance!" she heard Louis cry.

The next couple of minutes were like the climax of a nightmare to Amy. All she remembered afterwards was tearing at the bag, and it bursting open, and then plunging her hands into the slimy, smelly remains of Mum and Louis's pasta salad. And feeling around inside, like some revolting reality TV show challenge. And at last finding the batteries - right at the bottom - and running, still covered in mess, back to the living room where she had left the remote. And then the remote was sliding about in her hands as she tried to get the back off and remove the new batteries and replace the old ones...

"Call me from the hospital!" Louis was yelling. "Let me know!"

And then Amy was pushing past him, darting out into the street as the flashing blue light of the ambulance started to disappear, and aiming at her target as it moved further and further away, and, with all her might, pressing Mute…

And then, the ambulance, and Mum, and Dominic, were gone.

And Amy, in her night things, a slimy remote in her grubby hands, was standing with Louis on the doorstep.

Alone.

The wait that followed was one of the longest Amy had ever known.

She and Louis sat in the living room, watching the hands on the clock as they moved round from three to four. It was the first time Amy had ever been alone in a room with Louis, and there was an awkward silence.

"He'll be OK," Louis said eventually.

Amy managed a brief smile for him.

She couldn't stop looking at the remote, which lay once more on the table. Had she been fast enough? Had her aim been good enough? She wasn't even completely sure that she had pressed the right button.

She felt quite different about the remote now. Why had she been so excited? What had she been trying to do with her new toy? It had made everything seem possible.

Her eye fell upon the family portrait. Upon Dad. And she realised.

Not quite everything.

Louis saw where she was looking.

"I'm doing my best, y'know," he said abruptly.

Amy met his eyes. They were soft, brown eyes, and suddenly looked surprisingly warm and kind. Amy wondered why she hadn't seen that before.

The phone rang.

Both of them made a grab for it. Louis was fastest.

After an opening "Hello?" he said nothing. Amy had never seen him listen in silence for so long.

For a moment, her heart pounded.

Then Louis turned to her, and his stubbly face broke into a grin.

"He's fine."

"Absolutely fine." Mum was smiling on her return, much more than Amy had seen her smile in a long time. Dominic lay dozing in her arms, his thumb in his mouth. Louis took him from her very carefully. "Yeah. Just before we got there, he opened his mouth and cried. Didn't know where he was, I suppose, I've never been so pleased to hear him cry. Not since -" She paused, and avoided Louis's eye. "Not since the night he was born."

"Did they say what -" Louis started.

"Oh, I don't think they knew any more than we did." Mum was taking off her coat and was quickly getting back to her usual self. "But I made sure they checked him over, don't you worry. They said everything was fine."

"Amy and I were dead worried." Louis looked round. "Weren't we – Amy?"

But Amy wasn't there.

She was in the kitchen, at the sink, replacing the old batteries carefully in the bin.

"I've got to go in a minute," Adam said.

Sprawled out on his bed, Luke turned his head slightly to look at his friend.

"Huh?"

"Basketball." Adam got up from the red swivel chair in front of Luke's computer, where he had been sitting. "Starts at six. Got to get down the Leisure Centre."

"I thought it was aikido." Luke took a sweet from the bag next to him on the bed, threw it in the air and caught it expertly in his mouth.

"That was last night." Adam scrabbled around the tip that was Luke's room, moving smelly bits of laundry and boxed games, trying to find where he'd left his schoolbag. "Monday and Friday is Drama Club, Tuesday's aikido. Tonight it's basketball, tomorrow it's cornet."

"Busy life." Lying on his back, Luke was making his legs walk in mid-air, trying to see how far he could get his feet up the wall.

Adam's mobile beeped twice with a message alert.

"That'll be Mum." Adam fished out the phone and

opened the text. "She's at the end of the road, in the car. Better go."

"Have fun." Luke had got as far as he could up the wall and let his feet drop.

Adam grabbed his bag from on top of a pile of comics and headed for the door.

He paused for a moment and glanced at his friend. Luke's black hair was all sticking up. He still had his school uniform on, but his tie had found its way behind his left ear. He had the bag of candy on one side of him and an open packet of crisps on the other.

People, grown-ups, always said kids were lazy, never got out. Never got any exercise.

If they'd looked at Luke, Adam could have understood why.

It was for the same reason that Adam had started going to basketball.

"You need the exercise," Mum had said. And from that had come basketball, and football practice after school, and, in the summer, cricket. When Mum had read an article about how self-defence skills made kids safer on the streets, aikido had been added to the list as well. And when Adam's cousin Bethany had got the leading role in the school play, Adam had been signed up for Drama Club.

Luke never did anything, outside school. And not all that much in. Oh, he'd come out sometimes, kick a ball around. But he didn't do any clubs. When Adam was trying to throw somebody onto a rubber mat, or play in the key of F sharp, Luke would be comfortably slobbed out at home, with a big bar of fruit and nut chocolate, watching *Big Brother's Little Brother.*

How did he manage to stay so skinny?

"I'll see you tomorrow, then," Adam said.

"See you." Luke had two crisps in his mouth and was trying to make them into vampire's fangs.

Adam shook his head wearily and left.

A few hours later, Luke was still lying on his bed.

He'd finished all his snacks. And there was nothing much on TV.

Luke was becoming aware of an odd feeling. He felt...edgy. Annoyed. For once, he wasn't enjoying having nothing to do.

Was this what other people meant, when they said they were bored?

His phone beeped and he opened the text. It was from Adam. He'd just got home.

He didn't suppose Adam was ever bored. There was always something for him to do.

Luke blamed the parents. Adam's Mum arranged for him to do all those clubs and activities.

"You all right for a bit?" Luke's Mum had said, on Luke's return from school that afternoon. She was a hairdresser and had been styling old Mrs McIver from next door. The air had stunk of chemicals. "I'm off to do Maggie from Sansford, after this." She picked up the styling brush. "There's a couple of pasties you can microwave."

Luke looked back at the TV.

It was one of those reality shows. Two totally

different families, changing places for a few days, living each other's lives. Weird. But interesting…

It was then that Luke had the Idea.

"You're off your head," said Adam briefly, the next day. Luke had collared him in the playground, before school began. They were sitting on the old stretch of low wall at the edge of the yard.

"No, listen!" Luke sounded eager. "It's perfect. You're, like, dead stressed. And I'm bored having nothing to do. We just swap for a couple of days. You get to be me, take it easy. And I get to be you and go to all them clubs and stuff."

Adam stared at his friend. There were times when he thought Luke was just a bit crazy.

Could it work? The idea of a few days off being at clubs 'til eight, nine o'clock at night certainly sounded good. To come home from school and just slob around and watch telly.

"But how do we -" he started.

Luke gave him a cheeky grin.

"You just leave that to me."

"Yeah, OK." Luke's Mum shrugged. Luke had caught her just as she was off out to have her nails done, knowing that she wouldn't have time to argue. "You can have him to stay if you want. Long as he don't mind sharing with you." She sniffed. "You'd better tidy that room up first."

"When's he coming?" Adam's Mum demanded, at around the same time. She had been waxing the coffee table. "Don't forget you've got Drama Club tomorrow night. There's another rehearsal." She moved away to fetch a bowl of dried flowers.

"Tomorrow," Adam told her. "After school. It's cool, we can't start rehearsal 'til seven anyway, 'cause Alison's running it and she's going to get her boil lanced." He paused. "Luke's thinking of joining Drama Club anyway. He can come along with me."

"Very well." Adam's Mum arranged the flowers carefully in a central position. "As long as it's just for the weekend. And don't forget on Saturday you've got cricket practice." She moved to dust on top of the piano. "I don't want you spending the weekend just doing nothing."

Adam let her safely turn away before he grinned.

"What'd I tell you?" Luke crowed triumphantly.

It was Friday evening. They were both in Luke's room. Luke had decided to prepare for his visitor, and had arranged all his used socks neatly along the radiator. He had also left a pile of comics, fairly tidily, on the bed, and some packets of crisps and chocolate on the pillow.

"They never sussed."

"They probably will," Adam said pessimistically. Like a lot of plans, this scheme of Luke's suddenly felt much less fun now that it was actually about to start.

"Nah." Luke was looking quite smug at his success.

"I told you. 'Long as we get seen *together* now and then, there's no problem."

"Guess." Adam sounded far more nervous. "Just remember to keep in touch."

They paused, as there was a footstep on the landing outside.

The door opened, and Luke's Mum entered, carrying a tray. She set it down, as best she could, on the swivel chair. It was the only surface available.

There were two glasses of Coke and two plates of sandwiches.

"Hope sarnies are OK." She brushed her very blonde hair back from her face, and addressed Luke. "Your Dad's out the back working on his bike. I'm off out soon, to gym. You two going to be OK for a bit?"

"Yeah, sure." Luke smirked.

Luke's Mum viewed him doubtfully for a second. She knew that look.

There was the slightest hint of suspicion on her face as she closed the door.

"Better get off before her," Luke said. "Then she won't see me. My turn to be you." He turned to the tray. "And you get to be me. What's in 'em? Bet it's peanut butter again." He peeled back a slice of bread experimentally. "Yeah."

"Yeah, that is actually my tea now," Adam reminded him.

"Sorry." Luke put the slice back. "Anyway, she's made it for us both. So you get to eat two teas."

"See you tomorrow, then?" Adam asked.

"Yeah." Luke grabbed the Fax-R-Fab personal organiser he was using to map out their grand strategy. The whole plan was written in smudgy blue biro across the pages laid out for notes on *How I'm Going To Save The Environment*. "Checkpoint One is tomorrow, nine a.m. We meet at yours. Then we've got to leg it over here before Mum and Dad get up, so *they* see us both here for breakfast too. Good job your two get up early."

"We've got to fit Cricket in somehow," Adam reminded him.

"We will," Luke assured.

"And don't forget that rehearsal tonight," Adam said. "Remember what we agreed. And make sure you answer Mum's texts or she'll think something's wrong." He took the phone from his belt and handed it to Luke. "That's your lifeline."

"Relax, will you!" Luke demanded. "That's what you're here for." He grabbed the phone and stuffed it into his tracksuit jacket.

They paused. They were about to part, and it felt rather strange.

This was the first sleepover ever to be held in two different houses.

Then Luke smiled. "Have fun, Luke."

Adam returned the smile. "Cheers, Adam."

The door closed, a foot on the stair, and Luke was gone.

Adam waited a moment.

Then he switched on Luke's TV.

Grabbed the sandwiches and chocolate.

And, slowly, very satisfyingly, stretched out on the bed.

Yes!

Adam reached for another slab of chocolate, then paused.

He didn't really want it. He'd already eaten about three quarters of the big bar, along with both lots of sandwiches and all the crisps, and had swilled it all down with both big glasses of Coke, and was now starting to feel slightly sick.

He wondered what Mum had been cooking for tea. Busy every night he might have been, but he always had a hot meal first. Most nights, anyway.

He flicked through the channels on Luke's TV. Luke had digital. All those channels, and still there was nothing on.

The phone rang on the desk – Luke had his own phone, as well! – and Adam paused. The agreed signal was two rings. If it cut out after two –

It did.

He hopped up from the bed, moved to the phone and rang his own mobile, the one he'd given to Luke.

"Hey!" Luke sounded maddeningly happy. "How's it going, Luke?"

"It's all right." Adam tried not to sound grumpy. "How are you?"

"I'm good," Luke said. "Had my tea, round yours. Your Mum's food's *really* nice."

"What'd you have?" Adam asked, plaintively.

"Steak and kidney pie," Luke said cheerfully. "I never got that at home. Mashed potato, and carrot and swede – creamed up, you know? And *then* she'd made trifle! We were lucky. She had to go out, soon as she'd dished up, to see some old bat about the Ladies' Luncheon Club."

"Mrs Aspinall," Adam remembered. "The one with the two Airedales."

"So she doesn't know you didn't come for the food," Luke finished. "And I had your trifle as well." He paused. "How was your tea?"

"Great," said Adam acidly.

"Then I did your Drama Club," Luke said. "It's good fun. Don't know what you moan about. They liked me. They've given me a part in the play. I'm playing a tree."

"The environment play?" Adam's eyes widened. "I was in the Club nearly a year before they gave me a proper part in anything!"

"Ah, well." Adam could almost see Luke grinning, even over the phone. "You've got to get noticed in this life, mate. Anyway, I'll see you Checkpoint One tomorrow. Cheers!"

The line went dead.

Adam replaced the receiver in silence.

"Are you two up yet?"
Adam jumped. He leapt out of bed.
He looked at the diamond-shaped clock on the wall.
It was ten to nine!

He had to be at his house in ten minutes!

"If you want breakfast - "

Adam cringed. If Luke's Mum was making breakfast, she wouldn't need a knife, or any utensils. Her voice could have cut through anything.

"There's toast on, and jam and marmalade's in the fridge."

Adam found his voice, just.

"OK!" He fought to sound calm.

"Is Luke up?" Another shriek came.

Adam froze.

Then he had an inspiration.

He grabbed the pillow from the bed and shoved his face into it. Through the pillowcase, he gave a muffled shout.

"Yeah!"

"Oh, don't lie to me, Luke!" Luke's Mum didn't sound surprised. *"You're still in bed. I can hear you, I'm not daft! Get your backside up and get dressed! I've got to get down the Community Centre! I'm doing head massage this morning!"*

"Don't worry, Mrs Howard!" Adam's heart was thumping. Suppose she came in? "I'll see he does!"

There was sudden silence. A long pause.

Then Adam heard the front door close.

He breathed a sigh of relief.

He'd better go out the back way.

There wasn't time to do anything but change out of his night things into the t-shirt and tracksuit trousers he'd had on the night before. At home, he would have showered, put deodorant on, Mum would have had clean clothes ready for him. He was already in a sweat with the panic of all this, and the t-shirt was soon clinging to him horribly.

And this was meant to be a break!

He grabbed Luke's mobile from the bed and ran.

"Morning!" Luke was cheerfully stuffing down bacon and egg, when Adam arrived looking like a marathon runner who'd gone off course.

Wild-eyed, Adam collapsed into a kitchen chair.

Luke sniffed. "Did you shower this morning?"

"I overslept," Adam panted.

"No!" Luke sounded more amused than worried. "Did Mum and Dad catch you?"

"Your Mum's gone down the Community Centre." Adam put his hand to his head wearily. "Don't know where your Dad is."

"Probably out the back, doing something." Luke speared a grilled mushroom with his fork, and smeared it in the ketchup remaining on his plate. "We'd better get back there in a minute. We'll have to run."

Adam stared at him in horror.

The back door opened, and Adam's Mum entered.

"Saving the world is one thing," she said, more or less to herself. "But why we need three different coloured bins, I do not know." She caught sight of Adam. "Ah, you've finally condescended to get up. I thought you'd taken root in that bedroom. You ought to be up and about, getting exercise."

Adam gulped.

His mother sniffed.

"Did you shower this morning?" Another sniff answered her question. "Go and take a shower at once! And put some clean clothes on! I don't know what's the matter with you boys!" She paused, as if to reload with ammunition. "You'd better get going. Cricket practice starts in an hour. There's no time for you to laze around!"

With that, she turned and viciously started cleaning the sink.

Luke's grin disappeared as soon as he saw the look on Adam's face.

"I shouldn't be running straight out again!" Adam whined. "Not after a shower! It's cold! The sun's not out yet!"

He had showered and changed, too quickly to appreciate his own bathroom or his own wardrobe. Now he and Luke were running all the way back he had just come. Back to Luke's house.

"Oh, don't be such a girl!" Luke was faster, and Adam was struggling to keep pace with him. "We can't risk Dad missing us. We'll have to go to mine, have some toast. You can eat another breakfast, can't you?"

"I haven't had one yet!" Adam moaned.

"Then," Luke announced. "Cricket!" He paused, in mid-flight. "So, how d'you play the game again?"

"Checkpoint Two," Luke reminded. "After this."

They had arrived at the cricket ground in time for nets. Adam was batting, and Luke was proving remarkably quick in learning how to bowl. Not that he faced much of a challenge. Adam was too tired to pay much attention to the ball.

"We go back to yours." Luke delivered another ball, and Adam slashed at it resignedly. "Say how good cricket was, all that stuff. Then back to mine. So both the parents have seen us together a second time. You've got a treat in store, by the way. Mum's taking us out for a meal tonight, to the Ravenous Raven."

"Nice of her," Adam muttered dazedly. He had only had time to stuff down one slice of toast and margarine at Luke's, and was feeling far too empty to be playing sport.

"Not really." Luke smirked. "She just can't cook!" He paused. "Not like your Mum. Her fried bread this morning was just…Mmm!"

Adam gave him a murderous glare.

"Not bad." A tall figure cast a shadow across the cricket strip. It was Chris, a younger member of the adult cricket team who also ran the junior side. He had blond-dyed hair and a loud taste in tracksuits. "Luke, isn't it?"

"That's right," Luke answered.

"I've been watching from the pavilion," Chris continued. "Actually, we need a good bowler for the junior Second Eleven. We're playing the Chardwell lot in two weeks." He paused. "Don't suppose you'd be interested?"

Luke shrugged.

"Yeah."

"Cool!" Chris paused. "Watch the way you're holding that bat, Adam. It's not a shovel, y'know. You've been here long enough to know how to play the game properly."

He paused to give Luke a friendly pat on the back, then moved away.

Luke paused.

Chris was right.

Suddenly, he didn't like the way Adam was holding that bat either.

"I can't go on with this!" Adam whinged. It was evening. They were in Luke's room, changing, having both been ordered by Luke's Mum to put smarter gear on for the restaurant. Adam had just had time to grab his best shirt and trousers on their last visit to his own home. "I'm fed up with being you!" He paused. "And why are you so flaming good at being me?"

"Who knows!" Luke was still looking indecently cheerful. "Maybe I've always been talented. Maybe, somewhere deep inside, there's an achiever struggling to get out."

"Well, I've had enough of it!" Adam was in a real state, and his face was coming close to matching his mauve shirt. "Walking straight into Drama, and cricket, taking over. I've a good mind to go lazy for life!" He hesitated. "But I want to be it in my own house."

"Remember the deal," Luke reminded. "Sunday

night, that's what we agreed. Ready for us to be ourselves on Monday morning." He was backcombing his hair in front of the mirror, trying to look sophisticated. "Anyway, it's changed me, this. Done me good."

He turned to Adam.

"I think I might come to all your clubs from now on."

He ducked, and his neat hairstyle was suddenly destroyed, as a pillow narrowly missed his head. He glared aggressively.

"What?"

Like all family restaurants, the Ravenous Raven was packed on a Saturday evening. Adam, Luke and Luke's Mum had to stand and wait in the bar area to be allocated to a table. Luke's Dad had still been reassembling his bike and had refused to come.

"I can't believe how well it's all gone," Luke crowed. "Best plan of my life."

Adam said nothing. His eyes said it all.

"I feel like celebrating." Luke looked at the blackboard on which the daily specials were chalked. "I think I'll have a steak."

"I'm not hungry," Adam muttered.

"A whole weekend," Luke concluded. "With each other's parents. And none of them had any idea -"

"Ah!"

Adam and Luke turned.

And, as one, their blood ran cold.

Standing there were Adam's Mum and Dad.

"Surprise!" Adam's Dad beamed.

"We thought we'd just creep in," Adam's Mum explained. "It was quite out of the blue. Luke's mother rang and invited us to dinner. She said you were coming along here from Luke's house, after cricket. It's so kind of her, Luke. I suppose it's to say thanks for having you."

"Hiya!" Luke's Mum had turned to greet the new arrivals. "Good to see you."

"Haven't they found a table for us yet?" Adam's Dad was not one to wait. "I'll have a word at the bar."

"I might have a small sherry," said Adam's Mum, indulgently. She followed him.

Luke turned slowly to his mother, his eyes asking the question.

What did you do?

As if a mind-reader, she answered him.

"I thought we might as well get together." She shrugged, and flicked a lock of hair back from her heavily made-up eyes. "And it's a thank-you, of sorts. Luke's had stuff to do all weekend, Adam, thanks to you." She turned to a waiter who had approached them. "Any chance of that table by the clock, sweetheart?" She turned back to her son as the waiter moved off to check. "Dishy, isn't he?"

Luke was in no mood to answer.

As his Mum moved off towards the table, he remained where he was. He turned to Adam.

"If they get talking -?"

"And they will," Adam said.

Luke paused.

"I've gone off that steak."

"How far to the nearest chippy?" Adam said suddenly.

Luke paused. "'Bout five minutes. The Flying Fish. Greenfield Road…"

His eyes met Adam's.

"Come on!"

"OK, they've found one -" Luke's Mum had returned, and stopped suddenly as she found herself addressing the empty air. "Kids?"

"You know…" Luke gasped, as he and Adam sped in the direction of Greenfield Road. "That was a good plan of yours. Real quick."

He paused for breath, and glanced at his friend as they fled.

"Maybe you learned something from being me… after all."

Lunch

On the corner of the little street stood a lamppost. Once, men had come round every evening to light the gas lamp inside. But none came now.

The street itself was old, narrow, cobbled. The houses had been built in Victorian times. They were so small that they were barely big enough for a family of four to live in their cramped and dirty rooms, let alone the much bigger families still living there in the 1930s.

For a few minutes, late that morning, the whole place had lain deserted.

Then, along the cobbled street, Liam and Justin came.

They were carrying clipboards and had their rucksacks on their backs. They were followed by the rest of Juniper Class.

"Not bad, is it?" Justin asked his friend.

"Well." Liam shrugged. "If you like History."

An attendant in a black t-shirt hurried ahead of them to unlock a door just beyond the lamppost.

A moment later, they were back in the present day.

Liam and Justin sat down at a table in the Work Room to eat their lunch.

Just above them, the display board on the wall proclaimed:

"MUSEUM OF TWENTIETH CENTURY LIFE."

"What you got in yours?" asked Liam. They were taking plastic sandwich boxes out of their bags, like everyone else in the room.

Justin ripped the lid eagerly from his box.

"Can of Coke," he announced. He placed the can on the tabletop. "Cake. Crisps…"

"Beef and parsnip flavour?" Liam asked.

"Of course." Justin pulled the crisp packet open. "And I've got some chocolate…"

"No sandwiches?" Liam looked into the box.

"Nah." Justin sniffed. "Well, what's the point? I don't like 'em. Just something to get through before you get to the interesting stuff."

"Ah, you can't have a packed lunch without sarnies." Liam opened the foil-wrapped package he had taken out of his own box. He took out the first sandwich and groaned. "Ah, no."

"Ham?" Justin looked at the floppy purplish slice hanging out of the pieces of dry wholemeal bread.

"And cucumber," Liam moaned. He opened the sandwich up. "She knows I don't like cucumber."

"I'll have it." Justin reached across and plucked the cucumber from the sandwich.

"Hey!" Liam looked indignant at this invasion of his food. "Get your hands off! I've got to eat that sandwich!"

"Only trying to help." Justin popped the cucumber into his mouth.

Liam tutted.

He watched Justin's hands as they moved back to the crisps and the Coke can.

"Haven't you got brown hands?" he said suddenly.

"You what?" Justin swigged the Coke.

"Your hands," Liam repeated. "They're dead brown."

Justin looked at them with interest. He shrugged.

"Guess."

"You're always brown." Liam looked at his own hands, pasty white, slightly freckly. "Even in winter."

"That's 'cause I look like my Dad." Justin held the bag of crisps out to Liam, who took one. "My Dad's dead tanned."

"He's taller than you though," Liam pointed out. He looked at his friend. "And thinner."

Justin gave Liam a look.

"Cheers."

They went on with their food in silence for a short time.

"Don't you like this place, then?" Justin asked.

"S'all right." Liam was halfway through the second sandwich. He had taken the cucumber out and wrapped it in the silver foil. "Bit boring. They want to make it…what's-her-name…interactive."

"Mm," Justin agreed.

"Like," Liam went on. "In the war bit, you can hear all the bombs going off and everything. And a few people, dummies…But you don't see much. You could have a button to press, like. And everyone drops down dead."

"Yeah!" Justin enthused.

"Then there's Winston Churchill," Liam suggested. "'Stead of him just standing there. Have buttons on his waistcoat. Number one makes him talk. And number two makes smoke come out his cigar."

"Yeah," Justin agreed. He took a mouthful of Coke. "OK trip, though."

"Oh, yeah," Liam nodded.

There was another moment of silence.

Justin was picking at the top of the little iced cake he had brought, carefully removing the Smartie. "My sister made these."

"Yeah?" Liam crunched his apple.

"With my Nan." Justin swallowed the Smartie and bit into the cake.

"Weird what kids do," said Liam. "When they're little."

"They went on a trip," Justin said in an explosion of crumbs. Liam dodged. "Last week. The big museum. Not this one. The one near the Jolly Ferret pub."

"Oh yeah." Liam nodded.

"Doing the Egyptians," Justin went on. "I saw her drawing a picture after. She's a good drawer. There was a pyramid in bright yellow and she coloured the Ancient Egyptian in brown."

"Must've been one of your ancestors," Liam suggested. He sniggered. "Yeah! That's it! You're an Ancient Egyptian, J!"

There was a long silence, during which Justin looked bewildered.

"My Dad came from Ilford," he said eventually.

There was another silence.

Liam rolled his eyes.

Then the two of them returned in silence to their lunches.

"I haven't even answered half these questions." Justin flicked through the worksheets on his clipboard. "Where was the Great Depression Zone, anyway?"

"Just before the street," Liam answered. "The bit with all those fellas in flat caps queuing up for soup."

"All those poor people starving." Justin stuffed some chocolate into his mouth. "Horrible."

They fell silent once again.

"You coming fishing tomorrow, then?" Justin asked.

"Yeah." Liam nodded. "Come over. Mine. 'Bout eleven o'clock, twelve o'clock, something like that. Don't come any earlier, because tomorrow, I, will be having a lie-in. Followed by, a big breakfast." He leaned back in his chair with a satisfied smirk. "And then, a day's fishing."

"Hmm." Justin paused. "Liam?"

"Yeah?" Liam asked.

"Have you ever actually caught anything?"

There was silence for quite some time after that. Liam was rather coldly eating a muesli bar.

"I'm sick of all this health food crap," he said finally.

"Want some chocolate?" Justin held out what was left of the bar.

"Ta." Liam took a piece. He put it into his mouth, and instantly looked happier. "Ah, magic."

Justin had got the chocolate on his hands. He wiped them carelessly on his grey school trousers. He took a look around the room at their classmates.

"Was Sophie's hair always that colour?" he wondered.

"Nah." Liam finished the chocolate. "Had it dyed, didn't she?"

"I reckon Miss Hackett's had hers done too," Justin said. He looked round the room again. "Where is she?"

"Popped out for a fag," Liam said. "Left Jenkins in charge." He pointed out their own teacher, who was sitting on the other side of the room, looking stressed and eating a passion fruit yoghurt.

"The word on the street is, they're going out," Justin said matter-of-factly.

"You *what*?" Liam spluttered through an orange drink.

"Miss Hackett," Justin explained. "And Jenkins."

"*Them* two?" Liam gasped. "You're kidding."

"Nah," Justin insisted. "I got it off Kimberley. Her auntie works in that Bar and Grill near the station, you know, the Ravenous Raven. And she saw them in there together one night after school. They've got an Early Doors menu there."

"I don't believe it!" Liam was grinning.

"Oh yeah," Justin went on, "there's soup or a starter, and about six mains, and it's only nine ninety-five per…"

"I mean *them*, twit." Liam took a long, thoughtful sip of his drink, then smirked. "Jenkins and Miss Hackett! I'm keeping an eye on them."

"Reckon they're going to get married?" Justin asked.

"Nah," Liam said. "Too different, aren't they?"

"What d'you mean?" asked Justin.

"Well," Liam said. "Different lives. I mean, he does all the PE and Technology stuff, doesn't he? And she does Maths Group B. Wouldn't work."

"Ah, no," Justin agreed. He finished off his can of Coke.

There was another silence.

"OK, you lot!" Mr Jenkins called.

Miss Hackett had re-entered the room, but Mr Jenkins didn't look at her. Watching, Liam and Justin shook hands. They had this sussed.

"Finish off and put your stuff away! We're going now to the Welfare State Zone. And then it's back here to build those timelines!"

"Come on, then." Liam shoved his sandwich box into his bag. The rest of the class were also getting their things together, ready to move off.

Justin seemed to be deep in thought again.

"There's just one thing," he said finally.

"Yeah?" Liam asked.

"Well..." Justin wiped his hands again, this time on his sweater, then stared at them. "The Ancient Egyptians did all them...hieroglyphics. If that's where I came from...why aren't I better at drawing?"

Wish I Was There

"I'm going to Florida again," Amber said. She brushed a lock of her hair back behind her ear. "Going to do all the theme parks. Stay in a hotel." She leaned back in her chair. "We have to be up *so* early to go to the airport."

"We're going to France," Lauren said. "The South. My Dad knows someone who's letting us use their cottage. It's near a village where there's a café bar. And there's a cheese man comes round every week."

"Well, *we're* going on safari," Georgia announced.

"Whoa!" The other girls looked seriously impressed.

"In Africa." Georgia smiled triumphantly. "Kenya. They've got, like, these guides, who take you out in a jeep. And you get to see zebras. And lions."

"Mind they don't eat you." Amber sounded miffed.

"Where are *you* going, Emma?" Lauren asked.

There was silence.

Sitting opposite Georgia, Emma Reilly was looking down at the table.

"Yeah, where *are* you going?" Amber repeated. "You haven't even told me yet."

Again Emma said nothing.

She had been dreading for weeks this coming up. It was all right for the others. Georgia's parents had the money to take her on safari.

"You not going anywhere?" Georgia said, loud enough for the class next door to hear.

"'Course she is!" Amber said. "Aren't you, love?"

It was all right for Amber. Her Dad ran his own business.

"We can't afford to go abroad," Emma's Mum had said, again. "Money doesn't grow on trees, you know, babe. But your Auntie Sandra's invited us again. To Littlecombe."

Littlecombe might not have been so bad, thought Emma, if everyone else hadn't been going abroad. At least it was by the sea. And she'd have her cousin Katie for company.

But Littlecombe was in England. She'd be there in an English summer, which probably meant rain. And when everyone else was going to Florida, or Africa, or the South of France, and sent postcards with fancy foreign stamps, and came back suntanned…

"Where, then?" Georgia insisted.

"Spain." It was the first thing that came into Emma's head.

She was horrified as soon as she heard herself say it.

"Spain!" Amber sounded at least fairly impressed. "That's cool. Why didn't you tell me before?"

We've only just booked it.

"We've only just booked it," Emma said. "A last minute booking. On the Internet."

"I've been to Spain loads," Georgia said. "Whereabouts?"

Oh God.

"Marbella." Emma had heard the name on TV. She hoped desperately that it was in the right country.

"Hmm," Georgia replied grudgingly.

Yes. It was.

"Where are you going to stay?" Lauren asked.

Where were they going to stay. In Spain.

"A villa." Desperately, running out of ideas, Emma next stole one from Lauren. "We're borrowing it from someone my Mum knows."

"If you know them…" Georgia was sticking her nose in, as usual. "Why d'you need to book it on the Internet?"

There was a long silence. Then Emma gave up.

"I don't know. My Mum booked it."

"Hmm." Georgia smiled to herself, secretly, slyly.

Emma looked at Georgia nervously. Amber and Lauren believed her. But she had a horrible feeling Georgia didn't.

Georgia could never keep her big mouth shut. If she found out the lie… This could be really bad.

"I'll show you some photos of the villa tomorrow."

Again, Emma couldn't quite believe it was her own voice she could hear speaking.

"Oh." Georgia suddenly looked less smug. "OK."

That was something, anyway, Emma thought.

But what on earth was she doing to do now?

As soon as the bell rang, Emma ran.

"Don't forget those photos tomorrow!" Georgia called after her.

Emma's head was spinning.

There was no going back. She couldn't tell the girls that she'd made it all up, that she and her Mum weren't going to a sunny Spanish villa but to Littlecombe, probably with gales, and chip papers blowing along the promenade.

If she was going to survive, Emma needed photos. And fast.

Emma could only book the Internet for fifteen minutes in the local library.

Quickly, she hammered the word "Spain" into her search engine. Then she realised she'd have to say more. She added "Marbella", hoping it was spelt right, and then "villa".

When she saw what came up, and the prices, she nearly fainted.

She quickly moved her cursor away from "Book this" and up to "Print".

"That's dead nice." Lauren sounded envious the next morning. "Five minutes from the beach. Is that the view? Oh, that's gorgeous."

"It says this place sleeps ten," Georgia objected. "Thought there was only you and your Mum going. Bit expensive, isn't it?"

"They're borrowing it from someone, aren't they?" Amber pointed out. Emma could have hugged her.

For the time being, Georgia shut up.

They let it go for a bit after that. There was no more mention of Emma's holiday that day, or the next. And then suddenly it was the final week, with the end of term disco, and a picnic, and the last Assembly.

By the final day of term, Emma had almost forgotten about her lie. The printouts of the Spanish villa were squashed right down at the bottom of her schoolbag.

Then, just before hometime on the last day, when they were all waiting for the final bell like greyhounds awaiting the start of a race, Amber came up to Emma.

"So when are you off to Spain then?"

And Emma's heart sank.

"Monday." At least she had to give the real dates when she'd be away.

"I won't see you before, then." Amber gave Emma a big hug. "Have a good time. See you when you get back. And don't forget to send us a postcard, will you?"

Emma held on to Amber for dear life.

Over Amber's shoulder, she could see Georgia. And Georgia was smirking.

"This isn't too boring for you, love, is it?" Auntie Sandra asked at breakfast on the first day of Emma's holiday. She had cooked them all a huge meal of scrambled eggs, forgetting as usual that Emma didn't like them. Next to Emma at the round kitchen table with its checked cloth sat Katie, a year younger than Emma, stuffing herself with toast and Marmite.

"No," said Emma hastily.

She looked moodily out of the window. It wasn't raining. Yet. But the sky was cloudy and stormy. It wouldn't be long.

"We could go to the promenade after breakfast," said Katie, through Marmite.

Emma nodded.

She wondered what Amber was doing now. And Georgia. Georgia would be setting off for Africa in two weeks' time.

Emma walked down with Katie to the promenade. It was quite early and there weren't so many holidaymakers about yet. The funfair, with its brightly-coloured rides, wasn't yet open. The cafes, snack bars and amusement arcade were, and a few other kids were mooching about, buying hot dogs, or trying to get soft toys out of machines with the little mechanical cranes. And failing. Two older couples were walking along the seafront, beside the rough and choppy waters. A cool breeze was blowing off the sea onto the beach, and only the odd toddler had yet been brave enough to attempt a sandcastle.

It wasn't like the sign, thought Emma. The one she'd seen when Mum had driven into the town the day before. *Littlecombe extends a warm and sunny welcome to all its visitors.* Where was everyone?

There did seem to be a lot of traffic passing along the seafront though.

"They're all off to Buschels," Katie said.

"Uh?" Emma was thinking of Amber, getting ready to go to Florida in three weeks' time.

"The new supermarket," Katie said. "Opened just outside town. My friend's Mum has one of the shops on the prom, and she was so mad. All the people from the shops were. The supermarket's taking people away from them. And everybody drives there from, like, miles." She smiled. "I like it there though. The stuff's dead cheap. It's one of them foreign supermarkets. All foreign stuff you've never heard of. But it's cheap."

Emma stopped walking suddenly.

All at once, she thought she had an idea. Or the start of one…

"Can we go?" she said abruptly.

"You what?" Katie skidded to a halt.

"To that supermarket," Emma said.

"You want to go to Buschels?" Katie frowned.

"Well…" Emma thought fast. "You said it was good…and cheap."

"OK." Katie shrugged. "Guess we can walk there." She grinned. "Don't let 'em give you one of their stickers though. "I'VE BEEN TO BUSCHELS." I forgot, and I went into one of the shops on the front, and I was still wearing it. And everyone was like…" She opened her eyes wide in a terrifying glare. "Scary."

Ten minutes' walk brought them to the outskirts of town.

Buschels, Katie explained, had been built on the site of an old pub, the Ship, which had been knocked down. The Ship had once been a big part of life in Littlecombe.

That was another reason why the local people didn't like Buschels coming to town.

It was the typical modern glass-fronted supermarket, and its colours were scarlet and gold.

Katie wandered round after Emma, looking rather bored. She found some lollipops for them, and some makeup she wanted to buy.

Emma was interested in more unusual things. The foods at Buschels were certainly different. Or at least, the brand names were.

"What are you looking for, anyway?" Katie asked.

"Something for my friend Amber," Emma said. "Maybe my other friends too."

"There's all the gift shops on the front," Katie pointed out.

"No." Emma shook her head. "I want something... different." She spotted some biscuits. "How about those?"

"We bought some," Katie said. "They don't taste of anything."

Emma shrugged.

A few moments later, they were at the sweets and chocolates.

"Hey." Emma reached up to one of the higher shelves. "How about these?"

The chocolates were in a red and white box. The picture showed them - small, plain. Not very exciting-looking. But it was the name that interested Emma. *Bonbones.*

"What language is that?" Katie asked.

"Spanish." Emma smiled. "I think..." She took down

two more boxes of the chocolates from the shelf and headed for the checkout. "These'll do fine."

They had to queue for a few minutes. The shop was obviously much more popular with those not from the town.

The blonde woman in front of them didn't seem in any hurry. She was chatting to the woman serving at the till.

"You been away then?" she asked.

"Nah." The checkout lady was plump and middle-aged, with very frizzy brown hair. She had a deep, rather orange tan.

"Got the tan though," the blonde woman said.

"Just body lotion, innit?" The checkout lady grinned. "With a bit of fake tan. Rubs on each day. Good as the real thing. Everyone thinks you've been to the Costa Brava." She turned her attention to the next customers - Emma and Katie. "Hiya." She reached out a ring-covered and orange hand to swipe the girls' purchases through the till.

Emma was staring at the hand, and at the checkout lady's chubby face.

It didn't really look like a real suntan. But it wasn't bad...

"You just get it at the pharmacy," the checkout lady told the blonde woman. She looked at the readout on her till and turned back to the girls. "That's eleven ninety-eight, then."

"I don't get you." Back on the seafront, Katie walked along beside Emma. They were sucking their lollipops. "All that way and that's all you bought."

Emma didn't answer. She was staring out to sea.

The sky was still grey, and it didn't look as if she'd be coming back from this holiday with a tan.

But the checkout lady had given her an idea...

"Emma!" Katie yelled suddenly, but too late.

"Ow!" There was a cry.

Emma came back to reality to find she'd walked straight into a girl of about her own age, who had been making her way in the opposite direction along the promenade.

The girl had red hair. She looked mean. And very stroppy.

"Can't you look where you're going!" she snapped.

"Sorry." Emma backed off.

The red-haired girl tutted very loudly and dramatically, then moved off.

"Ow." Katie grinned. "You were, like, miles away then." She looked at her watch. "Coming to the arcade, then, or d'you want to go on the beach? Mum wants us back home for lunch at one o'clock, 'cause she's taking us to the Pavilion this afternoon for Summer Show." She rolled her eyes to Heaven. "She's been thinking up stuff to do with you for, like, weeks. Said she wanted to make it a real holiday for you." She moved on.

Emma lingered for a moment, staring down at the chewing gum and dog mess-covered ground.

As usual, the first two days of the holiday seemed very long, and the rest of the week seemed to fly by.

On Saturday, the final day, Auntie Sandra drove Katie, Emma and her Mum into Chardwell, the local market town. The adults allowed the girls to go off for a wander around the shops on their own.

It was then that Emma put the final phases of her plan into operation.

"There's some secret stuff I want to buy," she said mysteriously. She gave Katie as secret a smile as she could manage. "I'll see you at the tearoom in a bit."

"OK." Katie looked puzzled.

Once Katie had gone off to look in the video store, Emma made off quickly through the crowded streets. She'd seen the shop she wanted to visit on their way into the town.

Inside the pharmacy, Emma took a basket and made straight for the beauty products.

There it was. The stuff she wanted.

Body Lotion. With Self-Tanning Agent.

She popped it into her basket. Then she moved aisles, and found some fancy bubble bath for Auntie Sandra, and a lipstick for Katie.

It wasn't just that she wanted a reason for her "secret shopping". She really did want to thank her auntie and cousin for this holiday. Really, she wanted her family *and* friends to be pleased.

She went to the checkout, and stood behind people

buying sunscreen and sprays for wasp stings.

The price of her three items used up nearly all that was left of her holiday money.

To do the final bit, she had to move like lightning.

She was going to an Internet café she had spotted next door to the town's museum.

Once in the café, she booked fifteen minutes on the Net and searched for "Spain", "Marbella", "e-cards" and "postcards". There were hundreds of results, but she went for the first one. There was no time to lose.

Her screen quickly filled with images – sunburnt men standing by ancient gleaming white monuments, floral gardens bursting with colour. And beaches. Lots and lots of sun-drenched beaches.

With a pang of envy, Emma thought about what it would be like really to be there.

She chose the first image she found that had "Marbella" underneath it – an image of a gorgeous sunset of pink and blue and charcoal grey, enveloping a tropical-looking beach and cool rippling sea.

To make the image into a postcard, she had to sign up for the site. She gave as little information about herself as she could get away with. You had to be over eighteen to register, and she lied about her age, saying she was twenty.

Once the site had her card ready, she rattled off a message.

Hi Amber!!!

*Having a **luvvly** time in **gorgeous** sunshine. Great villa and great beach. We've done so much - tell u when I get back!! Say hi to Lauren (and Georgia…)*

Cu soon!!!!

Luv

Emma xxxxxxxxxxxxxxxx

That was all she had time for.

She hammered in Amber's e-mail address, then moved the cursor to "Send".

Once the card had gone, she logged off and ran as fast as she could back to the tearoom in the main street. Her shoulder bag felt heavier with her purchases from the pharmacy hidden inside.

She found Katie, Mum and Auntie Sandra waiting for her on the terrace, already surrounded by afternoon tea.

"Where did you get to?" Mum demanded.

"I went to e-mail Amber." Emma thought she might as well tell the truth about that, at least. She noticed Katie give her a funny look.

"You'll be *seeing* Amber next week." Mum gave Emma a look, then slid a plate over to her. "I saved you an iced bun."

"Cheers." Emma took the sticky cake and bit into it. Her face wore a grin of triumph.

The next day, before leaving, Emma gave Katie and Auntie Sandra their presents.

"Oh." Auntie Sandra smiled broadly. "Love." She gave Emma the sloppiest of kisses.

"I'm so going to miss you." Katie gave Emma a big hug, and whispered her final farewell into Emma's ear. "Even if you are a bit weird sometimes."

When they got home, there was an envelope addressed to Emma on the mat.

"Must have come by hand," Mum said. She looked round, looking slightly hassled. "That reminds me, I ought to go and get the post from Auntie May."

Auntie May was a lady down the road, who'd been looking after the house for them and taking their mail in while they were away.

"Will you be OK for a bit?" Mum asked.

Emma nodded.

Once the front door had closed behind Mum, Emma ran up to her bedroom.

She would be all right, for a short time. Auntie May always offered tea, and would want to know all about their holiday. Mum wouldn't be back just yet.

Leaving her envelope until later, Emma opened the soapbag she had taken as part of her luggage. The body lotion was inside, wrapped in her face flannel.

She read the instructions on the bottle quickly.

Apply daily… Wash hands thoroughly after applying.

Emma opened the bottle, squeezed out some of the

creamy white lotion and started to apply it to her face, arms and the backs of her hands.

It was just like sun lotion really. Although… She sniffed and frowned. It did have an odd smell. She'd need to put perfume or something on to disguise it.

Once the lotion was drying, Emma sat on her bed and ripped open the envelope.

It was a party invitation, written in Georgia's handwriting in red ink that looked like blood.

"Please come to my barbeque. My place. Saturday. From 4pm."

Twenty minutes later, Emma heard Mum come in downstairs.

"You all right, love?" she called up to Emma. "Sorry! Thought she'd keep me there forever. Got the mail. All bills. Fine thing to come back to…"

Emma got up from the bed and looked in the mirror.

God.

She'd gone orange.

She looked like a tangerine.

"You've caught the sun, haven't you?" Emma's Mum said at tea, over their fish fingers and peas. She frowned. "Funny. We had rotten weather most days."

For the next week, Emma went on putting the lotion on each day.

She was sick of it by the day of the barbeque. It really stank, and she was such a weird colour. She could have been the daughter of that checkout woman.

She'd kept out of Mum's way as much as possible, in case she guessed.

But everything had to look right.

Shortly before leaving for the barbeque, Emma put on a white top. She really wanted the other girls to see this tan. Not that they'd have much trouble.

Finally, she dug out the three boxes of *bonbones*.

This was it. Tonight was make or break time.

"Hey!" Amber came running across the lawn to Emma as soon as she entered Georgia's garden. "Did you have a good trip? Oh wow! You've got such a cool tan!" She embraced Emma, then frowned. "What's that smell?"

"New deodorant," Emma said quickly. "I'm going to change it."

"I got your card," Amber went on. "It was a good idea to send an e-card. You had Internet out there, then?"

"Yeah." Emma held out a paper bag. It had no logo on it. Nothing to show where the chocolates had come from. "I brought you these back."

"Oh, wow!" Amber opened the bag. "Thank you!"

She turned. Burgers were grilling on the barbeque, and there were drinks and crisps on a table in Georgia's parents' garden tent. Emma could see several of the class.

"Come on over!" Amber grabbed Emma's hand.

"Georgia and Lauren are over there. Tell us all about it! Georgia will be *so* jealous!"

"Jealous?" Emma asked.

"Well, didn't you know?" Amber grinned. "She's having this barbeque as a treat, 'cause her safari holiday had to be *cancelled!* Her Dad's work...They couldn't go! I saw her just after..." She stared at the clouds of smoke coming from the barbeque. "I think Georgia could be making that herself!"

"We went to the beach most days," Emma told the girls. "It was dead nice. Monday we did the Old Town – and the walls. The Moors built them, you know." She'd done her homework. That day, she had been back to the library, retraced the site where she had found the villa, and found out what were all the places to go and things to do nearby. "We saw the gardens, and one day we had a boat cruise. And then there was the villa, with its panoramic views, and every modern convenience." She thought maybe she should have put some of this into her own words. "Oh yeah – and another day we went on a trip. To Tangier."

Georgia was looking more and more put out with every second that passed, and was viciously eating a veggieburger.

"And we flew back Sunday," Emma finished. "It was *so* good." She smiled sweetly at Georgia.

"You've got a really good tan," Lauren said.

"And look what she got me." Amber showed off her *bonbones*. "All the way from Spain."

"I've got some for you too, Lauren," Emma said. "And you, Georgia. I didn't want you to think I'd forgotten you. On my holiday."

Finishing her burger, Georgia looked ready to choke.

Glowing with glee and her fake tan, Emma smiled to herself.

"All right, darling?" Georgia's Mum had appeared and was beaming for no apparent reason. "Look who's here!"

Georgia turned, and her face lit up.

"Poppy!" She moved over to hug the new arrival. "Hi! Oh, I haven't seen you for *ages*!" She addressed the other girls. "This is my friend Poppy. From Pony Club." She ushered her friend over to the other girls. "This is Emma."

Emma looked at the new arrival.

And her blood ran cold.

Standing as close as she had the week before, looking as mean as she had on the seafront at Littlecombe, the red-haired girl stared back at Emma.

The Tent

Jack was beginning to wish he'd never come.

It had seemed like such a cool idea. He himself had suggested it.

"Let's take the tent," he had said to Elliott enthusiastically. "And camp out, one night. No parents. No worries." And Elliott had agreed.

Now that they were there, Jack wasn't sure it had been such a good plan after all.

He certainly wasn't sure that it had been right to bring Sam, his little brother. Sam was a bit young to be doing things like that. But once Sam had heard of the planned trip, there had been no holding him back. After hours of *I want to come too*, it had seemed easier to say yes.

So there they were. The three of them. In the tent.

It was a good tent. Orange in colour. Big enough to hold the three of them quite comfortably – even taking into account a big boy like Elliott. Quite warm and cosy, and well-lit by the battery-operated camping lantern. It was a tent in which Jack had slept quite happily many times, on family camping holidays.

But Jack was quickly discovering that camping out

was very different when there were no adults around. The tent seemed different somehow. Slightly…lonely, in spite of Elliott and Sam being there. And slightly… spooky.

Was it just homesickness? Was he just missing the warmth and security of his own bed? Or was it also something else?

Could it have been…fear?

He knew that Sam was feeling it too. He looked at his brother, who was sitting nearby, his woolly hat pulled down over his forehead. Below the hat, his small, round face had the expression of one who was trying very hard to be brave, but starting to fail in the attempt. He looked like a frightened little gnome.

This was definitely not a trip for Sam.

It would have been easier if Elliott hadn't been doing his "tough guy" act, going on and on about how great it was to be camping out.

"Just us out here," he had said, shortly after they had put the tent up. "Us, against the rest of the world." He had paused, dramatically. "Surviving."

Elliott came out with a lot of stuff like that. He got it partly from Scouts and partly from watching all the survival challenge programmes on TV.

It was around that time that Jack had started to see Sam looking the way he did now.

Jack also wished Elliott wouldn't tease Sam. Elliott was a good mate really, but he did like taking the mickey out of people. Jack had seen him grinning when he had seen that Sam's sleeping bag had bunny rabbits on it. And when he had seen that Sam had brought a teddy.

Jack hoped that Elliott would remember that this was the first time that Sam had been out at night on his own, away from Mum and Dad.

It was getting darker outside. Soon, their only light would come from the lantern.

Jack shivered slightly.

"Cold?" Elliott looked at his friend.

"No," Jack said quickly.

"Or…" Elliott grinned. "You scared?"

Jack quickly shook his head. He wasn't going to have Elliott thinking he was afraid.

Elliott looked at Sam.

"How about you?"

"No." Sam's voice came out slightly squeaky.

"Nothing to be scared of." Elliott paused, then smiled, rather slyly. "Not 'til later. When it gets *really* dark."

Jack saw Sam's eyes widen. He quickly interrupted.

"Any more food?" He knew that question would distract Elliott.

"Think so…" Elliott had taken the bait. He reached for the rucksack and rummaged in it to see what was left of the picnic they had brought. "Few sandwiches. And a couple of apples…." He fished out a cheese sandwich that Jack and Sam's Mum had carefully wrapped in plastic film. He held it out to Jack in a rather grubby hand. "Want one?"

"Thanks." Jack took the sandwich and took a small bite. Eating would take his mind off things…for a bit.

"Have you got a drink?" Sam asked timidly.

"Yeah…" Elliott reached into the rucksack again and found a carton of orange juice.

"I'll do it for you," Jack offered. He took the drink from Elliott, removed the attached straw and poked it into the carton for Sam. He handed the drink to his little brother.

"Thank you," Sam said. Quietly, he took the drink.

Elliott took one of the apples and crunched it noisily.

They ate and drank for a few moments in silence.

Elliott looked up at the roof of the tent, in the direction of the sky.

"Be getting darker soon," he said.

Sam started looking uncomfortable again. Seeing this, Elliott was unable to resist teasing him further.

"Darker…" He assumed his spookiest expression, straight from the horror films he got his big brother to let him watch. "And ghostlier. And scarier…"

Sam turned worriedly towards Jack.

"And then…" Elliott shrank his voice to a whisper. "Who knows what might be waiting for us…out there… in the night!"

Sam grabbed his elder brother in panic.

"Elliott!" Jack had had enough of this. Elliott took this sort of thing too far, so that it stopped being funny. "Just leave him, will you?"

Elliott returned to his apple, grinning mischievously to himself.

Sam was still looking rather scared. Jack patted him reassuringly on the shoulder.

They continued their picnic.

Jack was still trying hard not to show it, but deep down, he was just as scared as Sam. It was getting very dark outside the tent now. And somehow…he felt chilly, even though they had chosen a warm night to camp out.

He looked at his watch.

There were hours to go until morning.

And eventually, they would all have to go to sleep. Out there alone. In the tent.

They would no longer know what might be about to happen to them.

The worst thing was that Elliott was right. It would be getting darker. And more frightening.

And how could they know, if anything were lurking out there in the night?

Waiting for them?

Time had passed.

The night was now at its darkest.

Only the lantern now lit the tent.

"Snap!" Elliott yelled – a bit too loudly, Jack thought.

Elliott had won again. He reached out and triumphantly gathered up the remaining cards.

The game was over.

It was Jack who had found the cards, buried deep in the rucksack. The game had been a good way to pass the time – and a good way to take his mind away from the darkening world outside the tent.

Snap was the only card game that Sam knew.

"Shall we play again?" Jack suggested eagerly.

Elliott yawned.

"I'm bored with that." He looked at his watch. "I'm tired."

Jack caught Sam's eye. They were both tired too, to tell the truth.

But neither of them was in any hurry to go to sleep.

"Bit early for bed, isn't it?" Jack asked. He made it sound like it would be a far more grown-up thing to stay up longer, knowing that this would appeal to Elliott.

Elliott shrugged.

"I guess… What shall we do, then?"

Jack struggled to think of some other way to pass the time.

"Hey. I know…" Elliott grinned. He had remembered the conversation earlier…and how easily he had been able to scare Sam. And it would be even easier to do so…now it was darker. "We could do what we do on Scout camp about this time. When it gets *really* dark, and we're all in the tent, like this." He paused mysteriously.

"What's that?" Sam asked timidly.

"We could…" Elliott paused again, and whispered his next words. "Tell a ghost story!"

Jack and Sam exchanged uneasy glances.

They didn't want to show it…but they were feeling nervous enough already.

And tales of ghosts wouldn't make them feel any better.

"I don't know…" Jack started.

"What's up?" Elliott gave a crafty grin. "You *are* scared, aren't you?"

"No," Jack said quickly.

"Well, then." Elliott smirked.

Jack hesitated.

The last thing he wanted in the world right now was a ghost story.

But if it meant losing face…and admitting he was scared…

Looking at Sam, he saw that his younger brother was thinking exactly the same.

He decided to compromise.

"Tell you what," he said awkwardly. "Let's get into our sleeping bags now." It would be cosier, and more reassuring, to be in the sleeping bags' warmth and comfort. It would probably be better for Sam as well. "Then…" he went on reluctantly. "You can tell us a story if you want."

A minute or so later, they were ready, sitting up in their sleeping bags. Sam sat there rather anxiously, surrounded by his bunnies. Jack had given his little brother his teddy, for extra comfort, and Sam was hugging it tightly.

Jack and Sam looked on expectantly.

Elliott was ready.

He hesitated for a moment before he began, enjoying their attention. Elliott loved an audience.

"It was a night just like this," he began quietly. "Dark…and spooky…and mysterious. And there was a group of people...out on a camping trip..."

Jack and Sam looked uneasy.

"Yeah," Elliott agreed. "Just like us. Out in a tent... with no one else near for miles around. Or..." He adopted his frightening look, and stared at Sam. "Was there?"

Sam squeezed the teddy tightly.

After a pause, Elliott went on with his story.

"They made themselves a meal. Cooked it over the campfire. Then, darkness fell. A terrible darkness. So dark, they couldn't see a thing. They settled down for the night."

Sam and Jack looked back at him.

"An hour passed," Elliott went on. "Maybe two. Then, one of the campers...the youngest one..." He looked straight at Sam, who shrank down into the sleeping bag. "He woke up...to hear...*something*... approaching the tent."

Sam's eyes widened.

"Something..." Elliott went on, "...*big*. He heard the sound as it came...slowly...and menacingly... towards him." He opened his mouth wide to increase the dramatic effect. "This was no human being. This was something altogether..." He allowed a scary expression to enter his eyes. "Different!"

Sam swallowed.

"He lay there," Elliott went on, "for what seemed like forever, until the beast, whatever it was, was right outside the tent. Then!"

He gasped.

Sam was starting to shake.

"He saw…" Elliott's voice shrank to a whisper. "*The tent-flap starting to open!*"

Sam blinked wildly.

"And suddenly…" Elliott continued. "Suddenly…"

All at once, he shot out a hand and grabbed Sam.

"ROAR!"

Sam shrieked and disappeared into the sleeping bag.

Elliott burst out laughing.

"Elliott!" Annoyed, Jack aimed a swipe at Elliott, who dodged, laughing all the while.

"Had you going!" Elliott's face was red from laughing so hard.

Jack looked concernedly at Sam, who was emerging from his hiding place, also looking rather red in the face.

"Right, that's it!" Jack had had enough of all this talk about ghosts and monsters. It wasn't making him feel much better than Sam. "We're going to sleep!" He flung himself down into a sleeping position.

"Suit yourself," Elliott said, rather grumpily. He'd thought it was quite a good joke. He couldn't see why Jack and Sam didn't want to share it. This camping trip was no fun.

"Hey." The voice was Sam's.

Jack sat up again, and he and Elliott looked at Sam.

"Isn't it…" Sam gulped. "Isn't it getting darker in here?"

Jack and Elliott exchanged glances.

Then they looked around the tent.

Sam was right.

It was.

Slowly, they all looked at the lantern, their only source of light.

The light was starting to fade.

All around them, the tent was being cast into shadows. The farthest corners, which had been brightly lit a short time before, were now dark and gloomy. The centre, where they sat, was shrouded in a dimmer, yellow light, a less powerful light – a light that was flickering.

And shadows were beginning to creep across their faces.

"It's happening!" Sam's voice was quiet, but terrified. "Darkness falling! Just like Elliott said!"

"Don't be stupid!" Jack came back sharply.

"It is!" Sam cried desperately. "Just like in the story!"

Jack looked around the tent in sudden fear.

He had already had to face the darkness falling outside the tent.

Now, there was darkness to face within.

For a moment, they stared at one another in horror.

Then, Jack looked at the lantern, and realised.

He made a sudden grab for it.

"You didn't change the batteries!" He glared at Elliott. "I thought you said you were going to put new ones in!"

"I thought you did!" Elliott snapped back.

"Oh, well, that's great, that is!" Jack glowered. "Out here in the dark, you getting us all spooked, and now we're going to have no light!"

"I thought you said you weren't scared!" Elliott retorted.

For a moment, they continued to stare at the fading light.

"We'll have to put it out," Elliott said eventually. He had quickly reassumed his position as the one who always knew what to do. "Put it out before we go to sleep. In case we need it in the night. We can't risk leaving it on and having it go out on us when we need it."

Jack frowned. This was brilliant. All of them shaken up by Elliott's stupid clowning…and now no light.

But Elliott was right…unfortunately.

They'd have to put the light out.

"Better get on with it then," he said reluctantly.

Slowly, the three of them settled down into their sleeping bags. Jack was the last.

He reached for the flickering lantern.

"Ready?" he asked.

After a moment's hesitation, he reached out and flicked the switch.

The tent was plunged into total darkness.

It was later. How much later, Jack didn't know. He couldn't see his watch in the dark.

He couldn't get to sleep.

Elliott had gone off some time ago. Jack knew that,

because Elliott snored. That was something else to annoy Jack.

He wasn't sure about Sam.

It was an odd feeling, lying there in the dark. Not knowing for sure how far the darkness extended around you, how far it was to the canvas walls of the tent.

And not knowing what might be lurking in the darkness outside.

Jack scowled to himself. Elliott and his stupid stories, getting them all nervous! Monsters lurking out in the night! What rubbish.

"Jack!"

Jack jumped.

Then he breathed a sigh of relief.

It was only Sam.

"What?" he asked, rather irritably.

"I can't sleep!" Sam's voice came plaintively out of the darkness.

Jack groaned inwardly.

"I keep thinking…" Sam went on. "About us lying here in the tent…and what could be out there…"

"Oh…" Jack was really annoyed now. "That's just Elliott winding you up…that's what he's like. Take no notice. Just go to sleep."

"I can't!" Sam insisted.

Jack took a deep breath. He couldn't very well tell Sam off for not being able to sleep, when neither could he.

He had to calm them both down…so they could get some rest.

Then he had a brainwave.

"Hang on, Sam," he said gently. "Look, tell you what. Lie back. Lie down. And get hold of Teddy. OK?"

"Yeah…" Sam's puzzled voice came back.

"OK." Jack paused. "Now…I'm going to tell you a story."

"I don't want another one!" Sam howled. Elliott's had been quite enough.

"You will," Jack replied, quite firmly. "Now…listen."

There was silence. Sam was listening.

Jack paused momentarily. Then he began his story.

"When I was your age…bit younger I suppose, I used to have this nightmare. This bad dream. In the dream, I was lying in bed, in the darkness…pretty much like we are now…when I heard this whining sound…coming from outside the window."

There was a rustling sound as Sam shrank down into the sleeping bag.

"And, in the dream…" Jack continued, "…I got up out of bed…and went to the window. The curtains were drawn…and I reached out…and pulled them back. And there…outside the window…was a face. A big, white, terrifying face!"

Sam gasped. Jack quickly moved on. Unlike Elliott, he wasn't trying to scare Sam.

"So…" Jack went on. "I used to lie awake every night…looking at the curtains…which were closed, just like they were in my dream…and be really, really scared. Because I thought the face was really there… outside the window…waiting for me to pull back the curtains. So it could get me.

'It went on…oh, must have been for weeks. I never mentioned it to Mum or Dad. You're the first one I've ever told.

'Then one night…I'd had enough. I was lying there…and suddenly I wasn't scared any more. Suddenly, I was going to see it…whatever might be outside the window.

'I got out of bed…just like in the dream…and went over to the curtains. And I grabbed them, and pulled them open. And do you know what I saw?"

There was silence from Sam.

"I saw this great view!" Jack explained. "Right across the town! All the houses, the church and everything… all lit up by the moon. It looked brilliant. And there was no sign of the face. Course there wasn't. It was all in my mind! Just a nasty dream. None of it was real at all."

He paused. He couldn't see Sam…yet he was sure his little brother was smiling.

"And it's the same with Elliott's stories," Jack finished. "All this stuff about things out there in the dark…it's just stupid. It only goes on inside our heads. And Elliott knows that too. That's why his daft stories worked…and why we were scared. It's all in our heads. And that's just stupid."

He paused for breath.

"Are you OK now?" he asked gently.

"Yeah," Sam's voice came back. He sounded quite happy. "Thanks, Jack."

"That's all right," Jack answered. "Now," he said quietly. "Let's go to sleep."

There was a rustling sound as the two of them settled down in their sleeping bags once more.

Jack smiled to himself in the darkness.

It had worked, just as he had hoped. The story had calmed them both down.

Now Jack was going to sleep, in case Sam realised that Jack had just made the whole tale up on the spur of the moment.

Elliott had been wrong. He wasn't the best storyteller in the tent.

Jack snuggled down in the sleeping bag, happy and relaxed once more, and ready to sleep.

Then he gave a yell, as something big and furry shot through the darkness and landed hard on his face.

Jack sat bolt upright in his sleeping bag.

Whatever had been on his face was suddenly gone…yet he could still feel the tingling that its fur had brought.

"What's happening?" Elliott was awake, shouting in the darkness.

There was another scream, from Sam.

"Sam?" Jack shouted. "What's going on?"

"Jack!" the small boy shrieked. "Jack, where are you?"

"What's going on?" Elliott bawled.

"There's something in here with us!" Jack was shaking. "I felt it…on my face!"

"It's here!" For the first time since they had entered

the tent, Elliott sounded really afraid. "It's next to me – ah!" He gave a sudden cry.

"What's happened?" Jack shouted.

"Oh!" Elliott gasped. "It's here! It's by me!"

"Where's the light?" Jack cried. "We've got to find the light!"

He felt round in the darkness frantically. His hands met the rucksack, the remains of their picnic...even the pack of cards...but no lantern.

Where was it?

He gasped.

The creature...whatever it was...had just brushed his hand with its fur.

He leapt back.

"It's there!" he shouted.

"Where *is* the light?" Elliott yelled back.

"I don't know!" Jack cried. "Help me find it!"

"*I'm* not!" Elliott sounded really scared now. "It's got me once already!"

"It's the monster!" A cry came from Sam. "Just like in the story! It's happening just like Elliott said!"

"Shut up!" Elliott cried. This was bad enough... without it being his fault. Actually, he had an awful feeling that it was. His story did seem to be coming true.

"Find that lantern!" Jack insisted. "Come on, help me!"

"Oh..." Elliott started to feel round the tent. His hand met whatever it was once more and he gave another cry.

"The lantern's not here!"

"It must be!" Jack retorted.

"Jack, I want to go home!" Sam's voice came. "Let me go home!"

"Be quiet!" Jack shouted. "And help us find it!"

There was silence as Sam started to help in the search for the lantern.

Then, the silence was broken.

A horrible, hissing sound filled the air. It grew louder…

There were two more cries of fear, one from Sam – and one from Elliott.

"What is it?" Elliott howled. "What is it? Oh!"

He cried out again. There was a pause, and then a crash. It sounded as if he had fallen backwards onto the tent floor.

"It's on me!" he shouted. "Get off me!" He addressed the unseen creature. "Get off me, get off!"

There was a loud hissing again, and then a scurrying sound as whatever it was came back across the tent.

"Keep it away from Sam!" Jack cried. He wasn't having his little brother in danger.

"Oh, I'm frightened!" Elliott's terrified voice came again. The tough guy of earlier, full of confidence and jokes, seemed to have vanished. "I want to get out of here! Where's the door?" There was the sound of him fumbling around the tent, trying to find the exit.

"Keep still!" Jack yelled. "Whatever it is, we don't want to get it angry! Now help me find that light!"

In desperation, the three of them tried to find the

lantern. They found the carton from Sam's drink, his teddy – which made them all yell again - and the cards, several times – but no lantern.

"Oh, I've had enough!" Elliott wailed. To hear his voice, you would have thought that he was younger than Sam. "I want to go home too!"

"Hang on!" Sam yelled. "I've got it!"

"Got it?" Elliott made a grab for the lantern in the darkness. There was a sudden crash.

"What's happened?" Jack shouted.

"I've dropped it!"

"Oh!" Jack exclaimed in fury. He reached down and found the lantern, rolling around the tent floor at his feet. He flicked the switch.

Nothing happened.

"Oh, Elliott!" Jack bellowed. "You've broken it!"

"Oh, I want to go!" Sam howled.

"Well, that's it!" Jack yelled. "That's our light gone!"

"Oh, I'm getting out of here!" The tent rocked as Elliott tried again to find the way out.

"Wait!" Sam cried. "I've just remembered something…before we came out…Mum gave me another torch!"

"What?" Jack cried.

"For emergencies!" Sam remembered. "The little torch of Dad's!"

"Well, where is it?" Jack asked.

"In the rucksack!"

All three of them made a grab for the rucksack.

The creature in the darkness was hissing again –

and as Elliott tried to find the rucksack, it brushed against him once more. He yelped.

"Hang on! I've found it!" Jack seized the rucksack and rummaged in it frantically. He found sandwich wrappers, apple cores, the wallet that still had the change from his school dinner money in it… "Where is it?"

"In the front!" Sam shouted. "The front pocket!"

Jack unzipped it quickly.

And there was the torch!

He flicked it on.

All three of them turned slowly as light filled the tent once more, to see what the creature was.

As one, the three boys cried out.

"A cat!"

A black and white cat looked back at them, hissing, tense and obviously just as frightened as they were.

"Go on! Shoo!" Jack could see the tent flap now. It was very slightly open. That was how the cat must have got in. He opened it wide. "Get out!"

Its escape route open, the cat fled.

The three boys paused.

Then they looked at one another.

Elliott stared at Jack and Sam.

Then he went bright red.

"Well…" he said defensively. "I didn't know what it was, did I?"

"No," Jack admitted. "Weird, though."

He gave a sudden grin, which Sam shared.

"I thought you were the one who was never scared."

Morning came – to the relief of all three of them. And perhaps also, to the relief of the cat.

Jack, Sam and Elliott sat up dozily, and struggled out of their sleeping bags. They yawned and stretched.

It was no longer dark, inside or outside the tent. The morning was fine, and brilliant sunshine gleamed its way through the tent flap.

Elliott was unusually quiet. Jack and Sam felt oddly cheerful.

"Sleep well?" Jack asked Sam.

"Fine." Sam smiled happily.

"Right then." Jack scrambled to his feet. "Let's go in. Mum said you could stay for breakfast, Ell."

Elliott cheered up at the mention of this.

Contentedly, the three campers stepped out of the tent, crossed Jack and Sam's garden and headed for the house.